"I don't apologize for what I want, and I always *get* what I want…and I want you. You should be flattered," Bastien told her without hesitation.

"I'm not flattered. I'm shocked and disgusted at your lack of scruples!" Lilah told him angrily, her blue eyes bright with condemnation. "You're trying to take advantage of this situation and play on my affection for my family."

"I will use any advantage I have and do whatever I have to do to win you," Bastien stated, his wide, beautifully shaped mouth firming as he stalked fluidly closer to tower over her. "You're the glittering prize here, Delilah. Doesn't that thrill you?"

Lilah stiffened even more. "No, of course it doesn't."

"It would thrill most women," Bastien told her drily, staring down at her with burnished dark golden eyes that sent an intoxicating fizz of awareness and frightening tension shooting through her every limb. "A woman likes to be wanted above all others."

"I very much ⬚⬚⬚⬚ that you're *capable* of wanting one woman ⬚⬚⬚⬚⬚⬚⬚⬚⬚⬚ retorted sharply.

"Sexual satis⬚⬚⬚⬚⬚⬚⬚⬚⬚⬚⬚⬚⬚⬚⬚ o me," Bastien par⬚⬚⬚⬚⬚⬚⬚⬚⬚⬚⬚⬚ity. "I don't feel⬚⬚⬚⬚⬚⬚⬚⬚⬚⬚⬚⬚ ologize for it."

Introducing Lynne Graham's fabulous new duet
full of prestige, power and passion!

These are two alpha males
you just *won't* be able to put down.

The Notorious Greeks

...and the women they claim!

Whether it is the boardroom or the bedroom
Leo and Bastien Zikos are masters of all that they
survey. Until they each meet a woman who has
the temerity to deny them the one thing
they most desperately crave...

In a true battle of wills, Graham whisks you away
to glamorous destinations and epic tales of love in:

The Greek Demands His Heir
August 2015

The Greek Commands His Mistress
September 2015

Lynne Graham

The Greek Commands
His Mistress

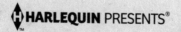

HARLEQUIN PRESENTS®

Recycling programs
for this product may
not exist in your area.

ISBN-13: 978-0-373-13367-3

The Greek Commands His Mistress

First North American Publication 2015

Copyright © 2015 by Lynne Graham

Printed in U.S.A.

www.Harlequin.com

Lynne Graham was born in Northern Ireland and has been a keen romance reader since her teens. She is very happily married, with an understanding husband who has learned to cook since she started to write! Her five children keep her on her toes. She has a very large dog who knocks everything over, a very small terrier who barks a lot, and two cats. When time allows, Lynne is a keen gardener.

Books by Lynne Graham

Harlequin Presents

The Secret His Mistress Carried
The Dimitrakos Proposition
A Ring to Secure His Heir
Unlocking Her Innocence

The Notorious Greeks

The Greek Demands His Heir

Bound by Gold

The Sheikh's Secret Babies
The Billionaire's Bridal Bargain

The Legacies of Powerful Men

Ravelli's Defiant Bride
Christakis's Rebellious Wife
Zarif's Convenient Queen

A Bride for a Billionaire

A Rich Man's Whim
The Sheikh's Prize
The Billionaire's Trophy
Challenging Dante

Visit the Author Profile page
at Harlequin.com for more titles.

CHAPTER ONE

'I'T'S OVER, REBA,' Bastien Zikos pronounced with finality.

The stunning blonde he was addressing flashed him a pained look of reproach. 'But we've been great together.'

'I've never pretended that this is anything more than it is…*sex*,' Bastien traded impatiently. 'Now we're done.'

Reba blinked rapidly, as though she was fighting back tears, but Bastien wasn't fooled. The only thing that would reduce Reba to tears would be a stingy pay-off. She was as hard as nails…and he was no more yielding. Indeed, when it came to women he was tough and cold. His mother, an eighteen-carat-gold-digging promiscuous shrew, with a polished line in fake tears and emotion, had been the first to teach her son distrust and contempt for her sex.

'You got bored with me, didn't you?' Reba condemned. 'I was warned that you had a short attention span. I should've listened.'

Impatience shivered through Bastien's very tall, muscular frame. Reba had been his mistress, and terrific entertainment in the bedroom, but it ended now.

And he had given her a small fortune in jewellery. He took nothing for free from women—not sex, not anything.

Bastien turned on his heel. 'My accountant will be in touch,' he said drily.

'There's someone else, isn't there?' the blonde snapped.

'If there is, it's none of your business,' Bastien told her icily, his dark eyes chilling in their detachment as he glanced back at her, his lean, extravagantly handsome features hard as iron.

His driver was waiting outside the building to ferry him to the airport for his scheduled flight north.

A very faint shadow of a smile softened the tough line of Bastien's mouth as he boarded his private jet. *Someone else?* Maybe…maybe not.

His finance director, Richard James, was already seated in the opulent cabin. 'Am I allowed to ask what secret allure—evidently known only to you—exists in this dull northern town we're heading to, and about the even more dull failed business enterprise you have recently acquired?'

'You can ask. I don't promise to answer,' Bastien traded, flicking lazily through the latest stock figures on his laptop.

'Then there *is* something special at Moore Components that I haven't yet picked up on?' the stocky blond man prompted ruefully. 'A patent? A new invention?'

Bastien dealt the other man a wryly amused glance. 'The factory is built on land worth millions,' he pointed out drily. 'A prime site for development close to the town centre.'

'It's been years since you played asset-stripper,'

Richard remarked in surprise, while Bastien's personal staff and his security team boarded at the rear of the cabin.

Bastien had started out buying and selling businesses and breaking them up to attain the maximum possible profit. He had no conscience about such things. Profit and loss was a fact of life in the business world. Trends came and went, as did contracts. Fortunes rose and fell as companies expanded and then contracted again.

Bastien was exceptionally gifted when it came to spotting trends and making millions. He had a mind like a steel trap and the fierce, aggressive drive of a male who had not had a wealthy family to give him his breaks. He was a self-made billionaire, who had started out with nothing, and he took great pride in his independence.

But just at that moment Bastien wasn't thinking about business. No, indeed. Bastien was thinking about Delilah Moore—the only woman who had ever rejected him, leaving him tormented by lust and outraged by the frustrating new experience. His ego would have withstood the rebuff had she been genuinely uninterested in him, but Bastien knew that had not been the case. He had seen the longing in her eyes, the telling tension of her body when she was close to him, had recognised the breathy intimate note in her voice.

He could forgive much, but unquestionably *not* her deceitful insistence that she didn't want him. Fearlessly and foolishly judgemental, she had flung Bastien's womanising reputation in his face with as much disdain as a fine lady dismissing the clumsy approaches of a street thug. In reaction, Bastien's rage had burned, and now, almost two years on, it was still smouldering at the lack of respect she had demonstrated—not to mention her lies and her sheer nerve in daring to attack him.

And now fortune had turned the tables on Delilah Moore and her family. Bastien savoured the fact with dark satisfaction. He didn't believe she would be hurling defiance at him this time around…

'How is he?' Lilah asked her stepmother in an undertone when she spotted her father, Robert, standing outside in the backyard of her small terraced house.

'Much the same…' Vickie, a small curvaceous blonde in her early thirties, groaned at the sink, where she was doing the dishes with a whinging toddler clinging to one leg. 'Of course he's depressed. He worked all his life to build up the firm and now it's gone. He feels like a failure, and being unable to get a job hasn't helped.'

'Hopefully something will come up soon,' Lilah pronounced with determined cheer as she scooped up her two-year-old half-sister Clara and settled her down with a toy to occupy her.

When life was challenging, Lilah was convinced that it was best to look for even the smallest reason to be glad and celebrate it. Just then she was busy reminding herself that, while her father *had* lost his business and his home, their family was still intact and they all had their health.

At the same time Lilah was marvelling at the reality that she had grown so close to the stepmother she had once loathed on sight. She had assumed that

Vickie was another one of the good-time girls her father had once specialised in, and only slowly had she come to recognise that, regardless of their twenty-year age gap, the couple were genuinely in love.

Her father and Vickie had married four years earlier and Lilah now had two half-siblings she adored: three-year-old Ben and little Clara.

Currently Lilah's family were sharing her own rented home. With only two small bedrooms, a cramped living room and an even tinier kitchen, it was a very tight squeeze. But until the council came up with alternative accommodation for her father and his family, or her father found a paying job, they didn't have much choice.

The impressive five-bedroom home that her father and his wife had once owned was gone now, along with the business. Everything had had to be sold to settle the loans her father had taken out in a desperate effort to keep Moore Components afloat.

'I'm still hoping that Bastien Zikos will throw your dad a lifeline,' Vickie confided in a sudden burst of optimism. 'I mean, nobody knows that business better than Robert, and surely there's a space somewhere in the office or the factory where your father could still make himself useful?'

Lilah resisted the urge to remark that Bastien was more likely to tie a concrete block to her father's leg and sink him. After all, the Greek billionaire had offered to buy Moore Components two years earlier and his offer had been refused. Her father should've sold up and got out then, she thought regretfully. But the business had been doing well and, although tempted by the offer, the older man had ultimately decided that he couldn't face stepping down.

It was no consolation to Lilah that Bastien himself had forecast disaster once he'd realised that the firm's prosperity depended on the retention of one very important contract. Within weeks of losing that contract Moore Components had been struggling to survive.

'I'd better get to work,' Lilah remarked in a brittle voice, bending down to pet the miniature dachshund pushing affectionately against her legs in the hope of getting some attention.

Since her family had moved in Skippy had been a little neglected, she conceded guiltily. When had she last taken him for anything other than the shortest of walks?

Thoroughly unsettled, however, by her stepmother's sanguine reference to Bastien Zikos as a possible saviour, Lilah abandoned Skippy to pull on her raincoat, knotting the belt at her narrow waist.

She was a small, slender woman, with long black hair and bright blue eyes. She was also one of the very few workers still actively employed at Moore Components now it had gone bust. The Official Receivers had come in, taken over and laid off most of the staff. Only the services of the human resources team had been retained, to deal with all the admin involved in closing down the business. Engaged to work just two more days there, Lilah knew that she too would soon be unemployed.

Vickie was already zipping Ben into his jacket, because Lilah left the little boy at nursery school on her way into work.

It was a brisk spring day, with a breeze, and constantly forced to claw her hair out of her eyes, Lilah regretted not having taken the time to put her hair up long before she dropped her little brother off at the school. Unfortunately she had been suffering sleepless nights and scrambling out of bed every morning heavy-eyed, running late.

Ever since she had learned that Bastien Zikos had bought her father's failed business she had been struggling to hide her apprehension. In that less-than-welcoming attitude to the new owner, however, Lilah stood very much alone. The Receivers had been ecstatic to find a buyer, while her father and various resident worthies had expressed the hope that the new owner would re-employ some of the people who had lost their jobs when Moore Components closed.

Only Lilah, who had once received a disturbing glimpse of the cold diamond-cutting strength of Bastien's ruthlessness, was full of pessimism and thought the prospect of Bastien arriving to break good news to the local community unlikely.

In fact, if ever a man could have been said to have *scared* Lilah, it was Bastien Zikos. Everything about the tall, amazingly handsome Greek had unnerved her. The way he looked, the way he talked, the domineering way he behaved. His whole attitude had been anathema to her and she had backed off fast—only to discover, to her dismay, that that kind of treatment only put Bastien into pursuit mode.

Although Lilah was only twenty-three she had distrusted self-assured, slick and handsome men all her life, fully convinced that most of them were lying, cheating players. After all, even her own father had once been like that—a serial adulterer whose affairs had caused her late mother great unhappiness.

Lilah didn't like to dwell on those traumatic years, when she had begun to hate her father, because it had seemed then that he could not be trusted with any woman—not her mother's friends, not even his office staff. Mercifully all that behaviour had stopped once her father met Vickie, and since then Lilah had contrived to forge a new and much closer relationship with her surviving parent. Only now Robert Moore had settled down was his daughter able to respect him again and forgive him for the past.

Bastien, on the other hand, was not the family-man type, and he had always enjoyed his bad reputation as a womaniser. He was an unashamed sexual predator, accustomed to reaching out and just taking any woman who took his fancy. He was rich, astute and incredibly good-looking. Women fell like ninepins around him, running to him the instant he crooked an inviting finger. But Lilah had run in the opposite direction, determined not to have her heart broken and her pride trampled by a man who only wanted her for her body.

She was worth more than that, she reminded herself staunchly, as she had done two years earlier—*much* more. She wanted a man who loved and cared about her and who would stick by her no matter what came their way.

Being powerfully attracted to a man like Bastien Zikos had been a living nightmare for Lilah, and she had refused to acknowledge her reaction to him or surrender to the temptation he provided. Yet even now, two years on, Lilah could still remember her first sight of him across a crowded auction room. Bastien…tall, dark and devastating, with his glorious black-lashed tawny eyes.

She had been there to view a pendant that had once belonged to her mother and which Vickie, unaware of Lilah's attachment to the piece, had put up for sale. Lilah had planned to buy it back quietly at auction, preferring that option to the challenge of telling Vickie that she had actually been pretty upset when her father had so thoughtlessly given all her late mother's jewellery to his then live-in girlfriend.

And the first person Lilah had seen that day had been Bastien, black hair falling over his brow, his bold bronzed profile taut as he examined something in his hand while an auction assistant in overalls stood by an open display cabinet. When she had been directed to that same cabinet she had been hugely taken aback to see that Bastien had had her mother's very ordinary silver sea horse pendant clasped in his lean brown hand.

'What are you doing with that?' she'd asked possessively.

'What's it to you?' Bastien had asked bluntly, glancing up and transfixing her with breathtaking dark brown eyes enhanced by lush, curling black lashes.

In that split second he had travelled in her estimation from merely handsome to utterly gorgeous, and her breath had tripped in her throat and her heart had started hammering—as if she stood on the edge of a dangerous precipice.

'It belonged to my mother.'

'Where did *she* get it from?' Bastien had shot at her, thoroughly disconcerting her.

'I was with her when she bought it at a car boot sale almost twenty years ago,' Lilah had confided. although she'd been startled by his question, not to mention the intensity of his appraisal.

'My mother lost it in London some time around then,' Bastien had mused in a dark, deep accented drawl that had sent odd little quivers travelling down her spine. He had turned over the pendant to display the engraving on the back, composed of two letter As enclosed in a heart shape. 'My father Anatole gave it to my mother Athene. What an extraordinary co-incidence that it should have belonged to *both* our mothers.'

'Extraordinary…' Lilah had agreed jerkily. as disturbed by his proximity as by his explanation. He'd been close enough that she'd been able to see the dark stubble shadowing his strong jawline and smell the citrus-sharp tenor of his cologne. Her nostrils had flared as she'd taken a hasty step backwards and cannoned into someone behind her.

Bastien had shot out a hand to steady her before she could stumble, long brown fingers closing round her narrow shoulder like a metal vice to keep her upright.

Lilah had jerked back again, breathless and flushed, heat flickering in places she had never felt warm before as her gaze had collided with the tall Greek's stunning eyes.

'May I see the pendant before it goes back in the cabinet?' she had asked curtly, putting out her hand.

'There's not much point in you looking at it. I'm planning to buy it,' Bastien had imparted drily.

Lilah's teeth had snapped together as though he had slapped her. 'So am I,' she had admitted grudgingly.

With reluctance Bastien had settled the pendant into her hand. Her eyes had prickled as she looked at it, because her mother had loved the fanciful piece and had often worn it in summer. The pendant reawakened a few of the happier memories of Lilah's childhood.

'Join me for coffee,' Bastien had urged, flipping the pendant back out of her hand to return it to the hovering assistant.

Lilah had dealt him a bemused look of surprise. 'It would hardly be a-appropriate,' she'd stammered. 'Not when we're both going to bid on the same lot.'

'Maybe I'm sentimental. Maybe I would like to hear about where the necklace has been all these years.'

Bastien had dangled that unlikely assurance in front of her like a prize carrot and she had caved in to coffee, feeling that to do otherwise would be rude and unreasonable.

And so her brief acquaintance with Bastien Zikos had begun, Lilah recalled unhappily. Hurriedly she blanked out the memories of that short week she never, *ever* allowed herself to think about, far too well aware of how mortifyingly long it was taking for her to forget meeting Bastien Zikos. Yet she had never had any regrets about turning him down—not then and not since, even when the most cursory internet search of Bastien's name always revealed the never-ending parade of different beauties that it took to keep Bastien happy. Quantity rather than quality was what Bastien went for in women, she had often thought, while telling herself that she had made the only decision she could…even if he still hated her for it.

As Lilah walked through the factory gates, saddened by the lack of vehicles and bustle that had used to characterise the once busy site, her mobile phone rang. Digging it out, she answered it. It was Josh, whom she had gone to university with, and he was suggesting she join him and a few friends for a night out. Every six weeks or so they met up as a group, went for a meal and out to see a film. One or two of the group were couples, the others simply friends. Josh, for example, was recovering from a broken engagement, and Lilah's last boyfriend had dumped her as soon as her father's business had hit the skids.

'Tomorrow night?' Lilah queried, thinking about it and liking the idea, because evenings in her crowded little house were currently far from relaxing and the idea of getting out was attractive. 'What time?'

Her friends would take her mind off things, she reflected gratefully, and stop her constantly fretting about a situation she had no control over. Unfortunately for Lilah an instinctive need to fix broken things and rescue people and animals ran deep and strong in her veins.

From the main office on the top floor, Bastien watched Delilah Moore cross the Moore Components car park with laser-sharp attention. She was still the most beautiful creature he had ever seen, he acknowledged, angry that that should *still* strike him as being the case. There had been a lot of women in his bed since he had met Robert Moore's daughter, but none of them had held his interest for very long.

Bastien still saw Delilah in the same light as he had first seen her, with her silky black curling cloud of hair falling almost to her waist and her sapphire-blue eyes electrifyingly noticeable against her creamy, perfect skin. Even wearing worn jeans and scuffed biker boots she'd had that casual effortlessly elegant look which some women had no matter what they wore.

Then, as now, he had told himself impatiently that she wasn't his type. With a single exception he had always gone for tall curvy blondes. Delilah was tiny, and very slender—the complete opposite of voluptuous. He just couldn't explain what made her so appealing to him, and that annoyed Bastien because *anything* he couldn't control or understand annoyed him.

This time around, he would get close enough to see all her flaws, he promised himself grimly.

'The new boss is in the building!' carolled Lilah's colleague Julie as soon as she walked into the small office the two women shared.

Halfway out of her coat, Lilah froze. 'When did he arrive?'

'The security guard said it was barely seven… talk about an early start!' Julie gushed admiringly. 'Mr Zikos has brought a whole team with him—I think that's hopeful, don't you? He is seriously good-looking too.'

Lilah's coat finally made it on to the hook. Her slender spine was rigid. *'Really?'*

'Absolutely beautiful…like a male supermodel. Maggie made coffee for him and even *she* agreed,' Julie said, referring to the office cleaner and tea lady, a known man-hater, who was hard to impress. 'But Maggie said it isn't his first visit. Apparently he was here a couple of years back?'

'Yes, he was. He was interested in buying this place then.'

'You *knew* that? You've seen him *before*?' Julie exclaimed in consternation. 'Why didn't you mention it?'

'With all that's been going on, it didn't seem important,' Lilah muttered, sitting down at her desk and closing her ears while Julie lamented her lack of interest in the new owner of Moore Components.

A young man with a neatly clipped beard entered their office an hour later. 'Miss Moore?' he asked, stopping in front of Lilah's desk. 'I'm one of Mr Zikos' team—Andreas Theodakis. Mr Zikos would like to see you in his office.'

Lilah lost colour and tried and failed to swallow, scolding herself for the instantaneous fear that washed through her. Of course Bastien wasn't going to harm her in any way. Why did even the thought of him charge her with near panic?

As she mounted the stairs she breathed slow and deep to compose herself. Bastien would want to crow, wouldn't he? He had got the business at a knockdown price and the Moore family had lost it, exactly as he had predicted. Rich, powerful men probably liked to boast whenever they got the opportunity, she reasoned uncertainly. For, really, her brain cried, what did *she* know about rich, powerful men? After all, Bastien was the only rich and powerful man she had ever met.

He was using her father's office, and it felt exceedingly strange to Lilah to be entering such a familiar space and find her father absent. Her eyes flickered super-fast over Bastien without pausing, as she registered that no other person was to be present for their meeting. Was that a good sign or a bad one?

'Mr Zikos,' she framed tightly.

'Oh. I think you can still call me Bastien,' he derided, studying her while wondering how on earth she could look so good in a plain black skirt of indeterminate length and a shapeless camel sweater.

Curly black hair lay in tumbled skeins across her shoulders. It was still the same length. He would have been vexed had she had it cut shorter. But, no, it was unchanged, and there was still something strangely fascinating about that long, long black hair that had ensnared his attention the instant he first saw it. And something equally memorable about the striking contrast between her bright blue eyes and her pale porcelain-fine skin.

Forced to look at him properly for the first time, Lilah froze, willing her rigid facial muscles to relax, ensuring that she betrayed no reaction to him. It was an exercise she had become adept at using in self-defence two years earlier. Her breath rattled in her throat, as if she had been dropped unexpectedly into a dark and haunted house where she was surrounded by unseen threats.

Bastien stood about six foot four inches tall, a clear twelve inches bigger than she was, which meant she could easily get away with focusing on his blue silk tie. But the glance she had got at him as she'd entered the office was still etched on her brain—as if it had been burned there in lines of fire with a red-hot poker. Whether she liked it or not, Julie had hit it right on the nail: Bastien *did* have a supermodel look, from his sculpted high cheekbones, classically arrogant nose and strong jawline to his full, incredibly kissable lips. Uncomfortable warmth washed up over her skin and she reddened, gritting her teeth, because she knew that she was blushing and that he would notice. *Why* would he notice? Because Bastien never missed a trick.

'Take a seat, Delilah…' Bastien indicated one of the armchairs beside the coffee table in one corner of the spacious panelled room.

'It's Lilah,' she corrected, and not for the first time.

He had always insisted on calling her by her full name—that name with its biblical connotations, which had caused her so much embarrassment from primary right up through to secondary school.

'I prefer *De*-lilah,' Bastien purred, with all the satisfaction of a jungle cat who had been lapping cream.

Lilah sank down in the chair, her slender spine too rigid to curve into the support of the seat. Her entire attention was locked on to Bastien and she clashed unwarily with his truly spectacular eyes. Tawny brown, golden in sunshine, literally mesmerising and surrounded by the most fabulous velvety black lashes, she reflected dizzily, plunged into one of the terrifying time-out-of-time lapses of concentration and discipline which Bastien had frequently inflicted on her two years earlier.

'I can't think why you would want to see me,' Lilah told him quietly, just as the door opened and Maggie bustled in with a tray of coffee and biscuits.

Lilah jumped up and immediately removed the tray from the older woman's grasp. Maggie had chosen to work well beyond retirement and, although she would never have admitted the fact, Maggie now found it difficult to carry heavy trays.

'I would've been fine,' Maggie scolded.

Lilah settled the tray of fancy silverware and fine china which her father's secretary had kept for VIPs down on the table. Maggie departed. Lilah poured the coffee and sugared Bastien's before she had even thought about what she was doing.

'You can't think why I would want to see you?' Bastien queried, unimpressed by the claim. 'How very modest you are...'

Suspecting him of mockery, Lilah flushed and extended his coffee to him. He reached for the cup and took a sip of the black, heavily sweetened coffee, smiling when he discovered that she had got it right.

Striving to play it cool and composed, Lilah lifted her own cup and saucer—but that smile...oh, *that* smile...was flipping up the corners of his beautiful mouth, transforming his lean, dark forbidding features with an almost boyish grin. Helplessly she stared, sapphire-blue eyes widening.

'Today,' Bastien drawled lazily, 'you are a very influential young woman, because it is in *your* power to decide what happens next to Moore Components.'

Lilah kept on staring at him, literally locked into immobility by that astonishing assurance. 'What on earth are you talking about?'

CHAPTER TWO

BASTIEN STUDIED HER, inordinate satisfaction glittering in his dark deep-set eyes. He had waited a long time for this particular moment and it was giving him even more of a kick than he had hoped.

'I have a few options to put before you. The fate of Moore Components is now entirely in your hands.'

Lilah set her coffee down with a jarring rattle of china and leapt upright. 'Why the heck would you say something like that to me?' she demanded.

'Because it's the truth. I don't lie and nor do I backtrack on promises,' Bastien asserted levelly. 'I assure you that what ultimately happens to this business will be solely *your* responsibility.'

Still frozen in place, Lilah blinked rapidly while she battled to concentrate. 'I don't understand. How can that be?'

'You're not that naïve,' Bastien drawled with a curled lip. 'You *know* I want you.'

'Still?' Lilah gasped in astonishment at that declaration, because after all two years had passed since their last meeting, and even six months on she would have expected Bastien barely to recall her name, never mind her face.

The faintest scoring of colour had flared across Bastien's high cheekbones and he parted his lips, even white teeth flashing. *'Still,'* he confirmed, with forbidding emphasis.

Lilah didn't understand how that was possible. How could he still find her attractive after all the other women he had been with in the intervening months? It didn't make sense to Lilah at all.

It was not as if she was some staggeringly beautiful woman who regularly stopped men dead in the street. Admittedly she had never had a problem attracting men, but retaining their interest when she wasn't prepared to slide casually into bed with them had proved much more of a challenge. In fact, most men walked away fast sooner than test her boundaries, choosing to assume that she was either devoutly religious or desirous of a wedding-ring-sized commitment before she would share her body.

Lilah dropped back into the seat she had vacated, her brain buzzing with bewildered thoughts. How could Bastien's continuing physical desire for her have anything to do with the business and its prospects? And how could he still find her attractive when he had so many other more sophisticated women in his life? Was it simply the fact that Lilah had once said no to him? Could a male as clever as Bastien be that outrageously basic?

'I don't want to keep you all morning, so I'll run through the three options.'

'Three…options…?' Lilah queried even more uneasily.

'Option one—you choose to walk away from me,' Bastien extended grimly, shooting her a glance of warning that made her pale. 'In that event I sell the machinery in the factory and sell the site to a developer. I already have a good offer for the land and it would turn an immediate healthy profit...'

Lilah dropped her head, appalled at that suggestion. The town needed this factory for employment. The closure of Moore Components had already damaged the small town's economy. Shops and entertainment venues were suffering from a downturn. People were struggling to find work because there were few other local jobs, and many had already had to put their houses up for sale because they could no longer afford their mortgages.

Lilah was well-acquainted with the human cost of unemployment and had done what little she could in her HR capacity to offer her father's former workers guidance and advise them on suitable retraining schemes.

'Option two—you choose only to spend *one* night with me,' Bastien framed, impervious to the slight sound Lilah made as her lips parted on a stricken gasp of disbelief. 'I will then make the business function again for at least a year. It will cost me money and it will be a waste of time, because the factory requires sustained and serious investment to win and retain new contracts. But if that's the best I can get from you I'm prepared to do it...'

Lilah lifted her head and focused on Bastien's lean darkly handsome face in sheer wonderment. 'Let me get this straight. You are using Moore Components as a means of bargaining with me for my *body*?' she spelled out incredulously. 'Are you out of your *mind*?'

'Be grateful. If I *didn't* want you there would be

nothing at all to put on the table. But for you I wouldn't even have bothered coming up here. I simply would have sold the land,' Bastien informed her with lethal cool.

Lilah had great difficulty hinging her jaw closed again, because she was stupefied by the options he was laying out before her. 'You can't possibly want me that much,' she told him involuntarily. 'That would be crazy.'

'Obviously I'm crazy.' Bastien dealt Lilah a slow, lingering appraisal that began at her lush pink lips, segued down to the small pert breasts outlined by her sweater and glossed over her delicately curved hipline to her shapely knees and ankles. 'You have terrific legs,' he mused, fighting the sting of awakening interest at his groin with fierce determination.

Two years back Delilah Moore had kept him in a state of virtually constant arousal that had given him sleepless nights and forced him into cold showers. He was damned if he was going to let her have that much of an effect on him again! He wanted her and that was that—but their affair would be on his terms only.

Option two was probably the wisest choice for him, because once he had bedded her, her fascination would surely wane fast and he would tire of her as he had tired of all her predecessors. But although he was convinced that one night should completely exorcise her from his fantasies, he still didn't want to be forced to agree to that restriction.

Lilah yanked her skirt down over her knees, suddenly boiling up below her clothing, her whole skin surface prickling and reacting to his visual assessment with a rush of heat. He was such a very sexual male, she conceded in bewilderment. The atmosphere pulsed with astonishing tension and she hurriedly snatched her attention from him, recognising the swelling tautness of her nipples and the surge of ungovernable heat between her thighs as totally unacceptable reactions.

But she couldn't prevent those reactions—couldn't stop them happening around Bastien. On that level two years earlier Bastien had drawn her like a moth to a flame, because the wild, seething excitement he'd evoked in her had been incredibly seductive.

In a desperate attempt to regain control of her disordered thoughts, Lilah said with careful precision, 'I refuse to believe you're serious about this, Bastien. A man of your stature and wealth cannot possibly want a woman like me so much that he would make such a bargain.'

'What would *you* know about it?' Bastien cut in, whiplash-abrupt in that dismissal. 'I haven't reached option three yet.'

Outraged by his persistence, Lilah rose to her feet again. 'I refuse to listen to any more of this nonsense!'

'Then I sell this place today,' Bastien fired at her with cold finality as she walked towards the door. 'Your choice, your decision, Delilah. You're lucky I'm giving you options.'

Lilah was still and then spun round again, black hair sliding in a glossy fall across her shoulders. *'Lucky?'* she exclaimed in angry disbelief, her temper stirring as she thought about the contemptible offer he had made to her. Bottom line: Bastien Zikos was willing to do just about anything to get her into bed. Was she supposed to be *pleased* about that? Was it normal to feel as insulted as she did…as *hurt*? Why did she feel hurt?

'With my backing you can wave a magic wand here and be a heroine if you want to be,' Bastien imparted very drily. 'Option three—I do almost anything you want, up to and including employing your father as consultant and manager.'

That startling suggestion not only stopped Lilah's thoughts mid-track and froze her feet to the carpet, it also made everything else inside her head blur. For a split second she pictured her deeply troubled father restored to some semblance of his former confident, energetic self, able to earn again and provide for his family. What a huge difference that would make to Robert Moore!

'So *that's* what it takes to stop you walking out… you're a real Daddy's girl!' Bastien remarked with galling amusement. 'Are you ready to listen now, and stop flouncing around dramatically and asking me if I'm crazy? The answer to that is that I'm only crazy to have you in my bed…'

Colour blossomed below Lilah's skin and ran up to her hairline in a scalding surge. She could barely credit that he had said that without even a shade of discomfiture. But then she reckoned it would take something considerably more shocking than sex to embarrass a male as resolute and dominant as Bastien. 'All right…for my father's sake I'll agree to hear you out,' she conceded with flat reluctance.

'Then *sit!*' Bastien indicated the chair.

It occurred to Lilah that Bastien had spoken to her just then as she spoke to Skippy when the dog was playing up.

Raising a wry brow at his disrespectful mode of addressing her, she sat down again. 'Option three?' she reminded him succinctly.

'You become my mistress and stay with me for as long as I want you.'

'Keeping a mistress is an astonishingly old-fashioned concept,' Lilah remarked, to mask the reality that inwardly she was knocked sideways by that proposition.

Bastien shifted a broad shoulder in a careless shrug. 'In my world it's the norm.'

'I assumed sex slavery of that sort ended about a hundred years ago.'

'But then you don't have a clue what the role entails,' Bastien said drily, watching her while picturing her slender body sheathed in decadent silk and lace and diamonds purely for his private enjoyment.

The image gave him both a high and a hard-on.

'In return for your agreement to become my mistress I will set this business up and invest in it. As the owner of a network of companies I can easily provide contracts to keep the factory busy. I will instruct your father to rehire his former workforce. After all, skilled employees are difficult to replace. With my full financial support, virtually everything could go back to the way it was before Moore Components lost that crucial contract.'

Lilah was floored by those comprehensive assurances. Now she understood Bastien's jibe about her having the opportunity to play the heroine and wave a magic wand. *Everything back the way it was!* How many times in recent months had she longed for that to happen and for everyone to be content again instead of stressed, broken and unhappy? Countless times.

Bastien was a very powerful, enormously wealthy male, and perhaps for the first time she fully appreciated that reality—because she knew it would take thousands and thousands of pounds to get the factory up and running again, never mind build the business up to survive in the long term. It would be a hugely expensive challenge, but it would turn around the lives of *so* many people, Lilah reflected with a sinking heart.

'Like Tinker Bell, you're quite taken with the offer of a magic wand?' Bastien quipped with brooding amusement as he watched her expressive face intently. 'I suppose your response will depend on how much of a do-gooder you are. So far you're ranging fairly high in that list of good works now that you have your whole family living with you. You're keeping them too, aren't you?'

Lilah was furious that he should have access to such facts about her personal life, and the label of 'do-gooder' offended her. 'I'm *not* a do-gooder.'

'By my estimation you are,' Bastien countered drily. 'You've saved your wicked stepmother from living in emergency accommodation and you also raise funds for abandoned dogs and starving children.'

Lilah stood up again in a sudden motion. 'How on earth do you know so much about me?'

'Obviously I've kept an eye on developments here.'

'My stepmother is *not* wicked,' Lilah added uncomfortably. 'How do you know my family are staying with me? How do you know about the volunteer work I've done for the dog sanctuary?'

'I had to check you out before I came up here,' Bastien pointed out impatiently. 'If you'd got married or picked up a boyfriend since we last met there would have been little point in my approaching you. I don't like to have my time wasted.'

Lilah's chin lifted. 'I *did* have a boyfriend!' she bit out resentfully.

'Not for very long. He dropped you the minute your father's business went down.'

Angry words brimmed on Lilah's tongue, but she swallowed them whole because she wasn't going to sink to the level of arguing with Bastien over someone as unworthy of her defence as Steve, her ex-boyfriend.

Ironically, Bastien's reading of Steve's behaviour exactly matched her own. Steve had turned out to be very ambitious. He had started dating Lilah when Moore Components was thriving and had tried to persuade her father to take him on as a junior partner. It mortified her that Bastien should know about the revealing speed and timing of Steve's defection.

Rigid with self-control, Lilah lifted her head high. 'I can't believe that you really mean those options you outlined. They're immoral.'

'I'm not a very moral man,' Bastien told her without hesitation. 'I don't apologise for what I want and I always *get* what I want…and I want you. You should be flattered.'

'I'm not flattered. I'm shocked and disgusted at your lack of scruple!' Lilah told him angrily, her blue eyes bright with condemnation. 'You're trying to take advantage of this situation and play on my affection for my family.'

'I will use any advantage I have and do whatever I have to do to win you. Of course whether or not you choose to accept one of my two preferred options is entirely your decision,' Bastien pointed out, his wide, beautifully shaped mouth firming as he stalked fluidly closer to tower over her. '*You're* the glittering prize here, Delilah. Doesn't that thrill you?'

Lilah stiffened even more. 'No, of course it doesn't.'

'It would thrill most women,' Bastien told her drily, staring down at her with burnished dark golden eyes that sent an intoxicating fizz of awareness and frightening tension shooting through her every limb. 'Most women like to be wanted above all others.'

'I very much doubt that you're *capable* of wanting one woman above all others,' Lilah retorted with sharp emphasis. 'Women seem to be very much interchangeable commodities to you, so I really can't understand why you should have a fixation about *me*.'

'It's *not* a fixation,' Bastien growled, dark eyes hard, strong jawline squared.

'Oh, for goodness' sake—call a spade a spade, Bastien!' Lilah countered in exasperation. 'At least look at the lengths you're willing to go to to *make* me do what you want...does that strike you as *normal*?'

'Sexual satisfaction is extremely important to me,' Bastien parried, studying her with cool gravity. 'I don't feel any need to explain that or to apologise for it.'

Lilah felt like someone beating her head up against a brick wall. Bastien didn't listen to what he didn't want to hear. He went full steam ahead, like an express train racing down a track. He saw what he wanted and he went for it, regardless of reason and the damage he might do.

'Delilah… I would treat you well…' Bastien murmured huskily.

'What you've suggested…it's out of the question—*impossible*!' she exclaimed in a furious outburst of frustration. 'Not to mention downright sleazy!'

Bastien lifted a lean tanned hand and scored a reproving fingertip along the strained line of her lush lower lip. 'I am never, *ever* sleazy…' He positively purred. 'You have a lot to learn about me.'

Subjected to even that minor physical contact, she felt her whole skin surface break out in enervated goose bumps and jerked back a hasty step.

'What I've learnt today, just listening to you, is more than enough,' she stressed in biting rejection. 'You talk as if you're playing some amusing game with me, but what you're proposing is offensive and unthinkable. And nothing you could hope to offer would persuade my father to accept a job that would literally sell me to the highest bidder as part of the deal!'

Bastien scanned her flushed and furious face and the sapphire-blue eyes shooting defiant sparks at him. 'Only an idiot would suggest that you tell your father the truth and nothing but the truth,' he derided. 'All you would need to tell your family is that I have offered you your dream job, which will entail a lot of foreign travel and an enviable lifestyle.'

With a reflexive little shudder at that Machiavellian suggestion, Lilah snapped, 'My goodness, you have absolutely everything worked out!'

'But will you take the bait?' Bastien breathed in a roughened undertone. 'You have until ten tomorrow morning to make your decision and choose an option.'

'You haven't given me even *one* reasonable or fair option,' Lilah condemned bitterly.

'If you don't give me your answer tomorrow I *will* sell,' Bastien warned her with chilling bite.

Her narrow spine went poker-straight with the force of her resentment and her slender hands knotted into fists. It was far from being the first time she had been in Bastien's company and had longed to knock his teeth down his throat.

In the smouldering silence, Bastien released his breath in a hiss of impatience. 'It doesn't have to be like this between us, Delilah. We could discuss this over dinner tonight.'

Lilah flung him a shaken and furious look over her shoulder as her perspiring hand worked frantically at the doorknob. 'Dinner? You've got to be joking! Anyway, I'm already booked,' she fibbed, refusing to give him the idea that she sat in every night.

'To see who?' Bastien demanded, pressing a hand against the door to prevent her from opening it.

'That's none of your business.' Refusing to fight for control of the door, Lilah stood back and folded her arms defensively. 'Nothing I do is any of your business. You may own Moore Components, but that's the only thing you own around here.'

Dark eyes glittering brilliant as stars, Bastien flung the door wide for her exit. 'I wouldn't be so sure of that, *koukla mou*.'

Lilah hurried downstairs and straight into the cloakroom, needing a moment before she returned to work and faced Julie and her curiosity. She was shaking and sweating, and she held her trembling hands below the cold tap while snatching in a deep sustaining breath, praying for self-control.

Unfortunately Bastien had struck her on her weakest flank. The very idea that she could rescue her family from their current predicament had turned her heart inside out with hope and desperation. And what about all the other people whose lives would be transformed by the opportunity to regain the jobs they had lost? Jobs in a revitalised business which would be much more secure with Bastien's backing? All their former workers would be ecstatic at the idea of the factory reopening.

But Bastien Zikos had put an incredibly high price on what that miracle would cost Lilah in personal terms. It was too much to think about, she thought weakly, anger still hurtling through her, tensing her every muscle. How could he *do* that? How could he stand there in front of her and outline such demeaning options? A one-night stand…or a one-night stand which ran and ran until he got bored? Some choice! What had she ever done to him to deserve such treatment?

Her temples thumped dully—a stress headache was forming. She was stressed, out of her depth and barely able to think straight, she acknowledged heavily. Hadn't she felt very much like that when she was first exposed to Bastien's soul-destroying charm?

Of course that charm had not been much in evidence just now, during their office meeting, she conceded bitterly. It had, however, been very much in evidence when Bastien had taken her for coffee at the auction house two years earlier.

After a casual exchange of names and information

Bastien had taken out his business card to show her that his company logo was, in fact, a seahorse. The awareness that he also had a strong family connection to the pendant had made Lilah relax more in his company. Noting his sleek gold Rolex watch, and the sharp tailoring of his stylish suit, she had recognised the hallmarks of wealth and suspected that it was highly unlikely that she could hope to outbid him at auction.

She had teased him about the amount of sugar he put in his coffee and a wickedly sensual smile had curved his lips, sending her heartbeat into overdrive. Oh, yes. At first sight she had been hugely, hopelessly attracted to Bastien and had hung on his every word.

'You still haven't explained one thing,' Bastien had mused. 'If you value it so much, why is the pendant being sold at auction?'

She had explained about the jewellery her father had given her stepmother. 'Now Vickie's having a big clean-out, and I didn't want to risk upsetting her by admitting how I felt.'

'If you don't ask, you don't get,' Bastien had censured drily. 'Not that I'm complaining. Your delicate sense of diplomacy has worked in *my* favour. If the necklace hadn't gone on sale I wouldn't have known where it was. I've been trying to track it down for years.'

'I suppose you remember your mother wearing it?' she remarked.

'No, but I remember my father giving it to her,' Bastien had countered rather bleakly, his dramatic dark eyes veiled while his beautiful mouth had tightened unexpectedly. 'I was about four years old and I honestly believed we were the perfect family.'

'Nothing wrong with that,' she had quipped with a big smile, trying to picture him as a little kid, thinking that he had probably been very cute, with a shock of black hair and brown eyes deep enough to drown in.

'Irrespective of what happens at the auction to-morrow, promise that you will have dinner with me tomorrow evening,' he'd urged, and had invited her to his hotel.

'I'm still planning to bid,' she warned him.

'I can afford to outbid most people. Dinner?' he'd pressed again.

And she had crumbled, like sand smoothed over and reshaped by a powerful wave.

Bastien hadn't made the connection between her and Moore Components, and it had been a big surprise for both of them when her auction disappointment had been followed by an unexpected meeting with Bastien in her father's office the next day. Dinner at Bastien's hotel had been replaced by dinner at her father's home, to which she had been invited as well.

When a phone call had claimed Robert Moore's attention he had asked his daughter to see Bastien out to his car.

'If you're expecting me to congratulate you on your win, you're destined for disappointment,' Lilah had warned Bastien on their way down the stairs. 'You paid a ludicrous amount for that pendant.'

Bastien laughed out loud. 'Says the woman who bidded me up to that ludicrous amount!'

Lilah reddened. 'Well, I had to at least *try* to get it. Why are you seeing my father?' she had asked abruptly as they came to a halt in the car park.

'I'm interested in acquiring his business and he

wants some time to think my offer over. You work here. *You* could be my acquisition too,' Bastien had said huskily, sexily in her ear, making the tiny hairs at her nape stand up while an arrow of heat shot straight down into her pelvis.

Unsettled by the strength of her reaction to him, Lilah had stiffened. 'I don't think so. I don't think Dad will sell up either—not when he's riding the crest of a wave.'

'That's the best time to sell.'

Bastien had dealt her a dark, lingering appraisal that had made her toes curl even as her gaze widened at the sight of the limousine that had rolled up to collect him. She'd been impressed but troubled by the obviously large difference in their financial status and had resolved to look him up on the internet as soon as she got the time.

'I wish your father hadn't invited us to his family dinner.' Bastien had sighed. 'I was looking forward to having you all to myself at my hotel.'

Unease had filtered through Lilah. He was coming on very strong, and while initially she'd been delighted by that, she was unnerved by the suspicion that he might be expecting her to spend the night with him. An impulsive move like that would have been way outside Lilah's comfort zone.

But at the same time still being a virgin at the age of twenty-one had not been part of Lilah's life plan either. She just hadn't met anyone at university who had attracted her enough to take that plunge. Lilah didn't give her trust easily to men, and by the end of first year, after standing by and watching friends commit too fast to casual relationships that had ended in tears and recriminations, she had decided that she would definitely hold off on sex until she met a man who cared enough about her to be prepared to wait until she was as ready for intimacy as he was.

'Bastien's really into you in a big way,' Vickie had whispered in amusement after dinner at her father's comfortable home that evening. 'He watches your every move. And although I prefer men to be more grey round the edges, he *is* gorgeous.'

Before Lilah had been able to call a taxi, Bastien had offered to run her home. Within seconds of them getting into the limo Bastien had reached for her with a determined hand and kissed her with a hungry, sensual ferocity that had set her treacherous body on fire. She had pulled back, trying to cool the moment down, but Bastien had ignored her.

'Spend the night with me,' he'd pressed, his thumb stroking her wrist where her pulse was racing insanely fast.

'I hardly know you,' she had pointed out hastily.

'You can get to know me in bed,' Bastien had quipped.

'That's not how I operate, Bastien,' Lilah had murmured, reddening with discomfiture. 'I would need to know you really well before I slept with you.'

'*Diavelos*... I'm only here for another forty-eight hours!' Bastien had ground out incredulously, studying her as though she was as strange and incongruous a sight as a snowball in the desert.

'I'm sorry. I can't change the way I am,' Lilah had told him quietly as the limousine drew up outside the terraced house where she lived.

'You're my polar opposite. I don't get to know

women really well. To be brutally honest, sex is the only intimacy I want or need,' Bastien had breathed in a driven undertone.

'We're like oil and water,' Lilah had mumbled, hurriedly vacating his car and heading indoors, to heave a sigh of relief as soon as the door was closed behind her.

In the aftermath of that uneasy parting tears had burned her eyes and she'd been immediately filled with self-loathing. She was guilty of having woven silly romantic dreams about Bastien. Hadn't she just got what she deserved for being so naïve? He was only interested in a night of casual sex—nothing more. It wasn't a compliment…it was a slap in the face—and a wake-up call to regain control of her wits.

Although Lilah had initially been attracted by Bastien's stunning good looks, she had been infinitely more fascinated by his strong personality, and the seemingly offbeat way his brain worked. That same night she'd sat up late, looking Bastien up on the internet, and the sheer number of women she'd seen pictured with him had shaken her almost as much as his reputation for being a womaniser. Bastien Zikos slept around and he was faithless.

At first Lilah had been appalled by what she had discovered, but there had also been an oddly soothing element to those revelations. After all, what she had found out only emphasised that she could never have any kind of liaison with Bastien: he didn't do relationships…and she didn't do one-night stands.

Sinking back to the present, Lilah was dismayed to register that her eyes were swimming with tears. She blinked them back and freshened up, writing off her far too emotional frame of mind to the shocks Bastien had dealt her. She hated the way that Bastien always got to her—cutting through her common sense and reserve like a machete to make his forceful point.

'You were a long time upstairs with the boss,' Julie commented as Lilah dropped back behind her desk.

'Mr Zikos wanted to discuss his plans for the business,' she said awkwardly.

'Oh...*wow*!' Julie gushed, fixing wide, speculative eyes on Lilah's flushed and taut face. 'You mean he's planning to keep Moore Components open? He's not just going to sell up?'

Lilah cursed her loose tongue. 'No, his selling up is a possibility too,' she backtracked hastily, fearful of setting off a round of rumours that would raise false hopes. 'I don't think he's actually made a final decision yet.'

With a regretful sigh, Julie returned to work. But Lilah found that she could not concentrate for longer than thirty seconds. Aftershocks from her meeting with Bastien were still quaking through her.

He might as well have taken the moon down from the sky and offered it to her, she reflected in a daze. Her family were suffering—just like everybody else caught up in the crash of Moore Components. The little half-brother and half-sister so dear to Lilah's heart no longer had a garden to play in, and their more elaborate toys had been disposed of because there was no room for such things in Lilah's little house. Her father was suffering from depression and taking medication. The day the factory had closed the bottom had dropped out of his world. Without work, without his business, Robert Moore simply didn't know what to do with himself.

Lilah blinked back stinging tears. In spite of the troubled years, when her parents had been unhappily married, Lilah still loved her father very much. She had only been eleven years old when her mother had died very suddenly from an aneurysm. Her father had been very much there for her while she was grieving, but he was also a very hard worker, who had soon returned to work, slaving eighteen hours a day to build up his business.

Now, shorn of his once generous income and humbled, he felt less of a man—and at his age, with a failed business under his belt, who was likely to employ him? Although Lilah had told herself that she shouldn't be thinking about it, she could not resist picturing her father returning to work with a new spring in his step.

She blanked out the thought.

Was she really prepared to become a mistress?

Bastien's sex slave?

An extraordinary little chirrup of excitement twisted through Lilah and she was seriously embarrassed for herself. She was pretty sure Bastien wouldn't be expecting a virgin. But what did that matter? It was not as though she was seriously considering his sordid options, was it?

Still mentally far removed from work, she sank back two years again into her memories and recalled the flowers Bastien had sent her the morning after that family dinner and her rejection of what little he'd had to offer her. He had shown up on her doorstep the following evening as well, displaying a persistence that had taxed her patience. When he had tried to persuade her to join him that night for dinner she had lost her temper with him.

Why had she lost her temper?

Remembering why, Lilah paled and then flushed a painful pink. Utterly mesmerised by Bastien, she had already started falling for him. Being rudely confronted with the reality that he was a stud, who only wanted her for sex, had been hurtful and demeaning. *That* was why she had lost her temper. She had been angry with herself because somehow he had contrived to tempt her with that single erotically charged kiss and had made her question her own values. She had resented his power over her and she had flung her knowledge of his bad reputation in his teeth and called him a man whore.

Lilah was still secretly cringing from that memory as she walked home after work. Attacking Bastien had been wrong. He was what he was, and she was what she was. They were very different people. Insulting him had been ill-mannered, pointless and immature. His dark eyes had glittered like black ice, the rage in his stunning gaze filling her with fright. But he had done nothing, said nothing. He had simply turned on his heel and got back into his opulent limousine to drive away.

A few weeks later an unexpected gift had arrived for her at work. She had unwrapped an almost exact replica of the seahorse pendant Bastien had won at auction. The only difference between it and the original was that the new piece lacked the engraved initial As on the back. Only Bastien could have had it made for her and sent it to her. That he had given the pendant to her in spite of the way she had spoken to him had shocked Lilah, and made her feel as if she didn't know Bastien Zikos at all. She had asked herself then if she had imagined that dark fury in his eyes.

But now Lilah knew for a fact that she had not imagined Bastien's rage, and she suspected that what she was being subjected to was 'payback time' in his parlance.

CHAPTER THREE

IN THE MIDDLE of the night, tossing and turning without sleep, Lilah crept out of bed and went downstairs to make herself a cup of tea.

Vickie was already there, seated at the kitchen table. 'Great minds, eh?' she framed round a huge yawn.

'You couldn't sleep either?' Lilah stated the obvious.

'It's the constant worrying that keeps me awake,' her father's wife opined ruefully while Lilah boiled the kettle. 'Some of the parents I was talking to at Ben's school said Bastien Zikos was at Moore Components today... I was surprised you hadn't mentioned it.'

Lilah stiffened defensively. 'I didn't see the point.'

'I hate asking you this...but I was thinking...maybe if you get the chance you could ask Bastien if he has an opening for your father anywhere?' Vickie said hopefully.

Lilah reddened. 'If I get the chance,' she echoed, feeling incredibly guilty for not telling the truth.

Bastien had been right on that score. No one would thank her for telling a truth that no one wanted to hear. And the truth was that she *could* wave a magic wand

and fix everything for everybody. How could she live with that knowledge and stand by doing nothing? How could she live with seeing her father slumped in a chair, staring into space? It was all very well to be furious with Bastien, to take offence and walk out. but at the end of the day she had to be practical. He had, after all, offered her a miracle.

Everything back the way it was.

Hanging on to her virginity at all costs seemed a little pathetic in such dire circumstances, didn't it? And, whether she liked it or not, she had always been attracted to Bastien. How could she hold out and justify herself when so many positive outcomes would result from her agreement? Bastien's interest in her would be short-lived as well: his past history spoke for him. He never stayed long with a woman. She would get her life back again quickly and probably never come back home, she acknowledged unhappily. When Bastien got bored with her she would look for a job in London and make a fresh start.

Lilah dressed for work with more care than usual, braiding her black mane of hair into submission and choosing a black pencil skirt and a silky cream blouse to wear.

The mere thought of finding herself in bed with Bastien brought her out in a cold sweat and turned her tummy over, so she refused to think about it. Sex was a rite of passage, she told herself impatiently. She was no different from any other woman and would soon become accustomed to it. No doubt practise had made Bastien most proficient in that department, and it was probably safe to assume that she wouldn't find sharing a bed with him too unpleasant. Of course she wasn't going to *enjoy* any of it either. Sex shorn of any finer feelings was a physical rather than mental exercise and she would detach herself from the whole experience, she told herself soothingly.

Detachment, after all, would hardly be a challenge when she hated Bastien with every fibre of her being. His options had taught her to hate him. Before yesterday he had simply been the womaniser who had once bruised her tender heart and whom she couldn't ever have. Now he was the ruthless lowlife forcing her to seal a bargain with her body as if she was a whore.

A little shudder racked her at that view and she breathed in slow and deep, strengthening herself for what lay ahead. She was about to make a devil's bargain, but she was darned if she would show an ounce of weakness in front of Bastien.

When she walked into the office, Julie gave her a curious appraisal. 'Mr Zikos has phoned down to ask for you already. I explained that you're never in before nine because you leave your kid brother at nursery on the way.'

'Thanks,' Lilah breathed, hanging up her coat with a nervous hand.

Bastien had said ten o'clock, but he was clearly jumping the gun. Of course he had no patience whatsoever, she reflected ruefully. He tapped his feet and drummed his fingers when forced to be inactive for any length of time. He was edgy, bursting with frenetic energy, always in need of occupation.

She smoothed her skirt down over her hips as she mounted the stairs. Her hands weren't quite steady and she studied them in dismay. Why was she getting

herself into a state? Hadn't she already decided that
sex would be no big deal and not worth making a silly
fuss over? It wasn't as though Bastien was going to
spread her across the office desk and have his wicked
way with her this very day…was it?

Her face burned, her stomach performing a somersault at that X-rated image. She wanted Bastien to
do the deed in pitch-darkness and complete silence.
She didn't want to have to look at him or speak to
him. She wished there was some way of having sex
remotely, without any need for physical contact, and
it was on that crazy thought that she entered what had
once been her father's office.

With a single gesture Bastien dismissed the team
hovering attentively round him and set down the tablet he had been studying.

'You've asked for me but it's not ten yet,' Lilah
pointed out thinly. 'It's only ten minutes past nine.'

Bastien straightened, brilliant dark golden eyes
lancing into hers in direct challenge. 'My internal
clock says it's ten,' he contradicted without hesitation.

'Your clock's wrong.'

'I'm *never* wrong, Delilah,' Bastien traded thickly,
his long-lashed gaze roaming over her as intently as
a physical caress. 'Lesson one on how to be a mistress: I keep you around to stroke my ego, not dent it.'

Lilah froze where she stood, wide sapphire eyes
travelling over him with a hunger she couldn't control. She scanned the exquisitely tailored designer suit
that delineated every muscular line of Bastien's broad-
shouldered, lean-hipped frame as he stood there facing
her, with his long, powerful legs braced. Something

clenched low in her body when she clashed with his gaze and her legs felt strangely hollow.

Her attention welded to his darkly handsome face, she stopped breathing, reacting with dismay to the treacherous stirrings of her own body. Her breasts swelled, constrained by the confines of her bra, while the sensation at her feminine core made her press her thighs together hard.

'I'm no good at stroking egos, Bastien,' she warned him.

Bastien dealt her an unholy grin. 'I've got enough ego to survive a few dents,' he asserted. 'Where do you think your true talents will lie?'

'You've taken my answer for granted, haven't you?' Lilah exclaimed. 'I haven't said yes yet, but you're convinced I will.'

'And am I wrong?' Bastien traded.

Her teeth gritted together. 'No, you're not.'

'So, are you going for option two or option three?' Bastien enquired lazily, leaning back against his desk in an attitude of relaxation that infuriated her.

Option three, option *three*, Bastien willed Delilah to tell him. That would be the most profitable option for him. He would sell the current site, relocate the factory to the outskirts of town and in doing so take advantage of several lucrative government grants aimed at persuading companies to open up in areas of high unemployment. For him it would be a win-win situation, because he would gain Lilah, an immediate profit to cover all outlay *and* a cost-efficient business.

'You have no shame, have you?' Lilah hissed, like oil bubbling on too high a heat.

'Not when it comes to you,' Bastien agreed. 'It's the only way I'm ever going to get you, because you're stubborn and contrary and you have a very closed little mind.'

'I am none of those things,' Lilah rebutted angrily.

'Stubborn because the minute we saw each other we were destined to be together but you immediately fought it. Contrary because you feel the same way about me as I do about you—instantaneous lust—but you deny it. And a closed mind because you believe a life of self-denial is innately superior to mine.' A wolfish smile slashed Bastien's lean strong face. 'I can't wait for the moment when you realise that you can't keep your hands off me.'

Lilah gave him a look of withering scorn. 'You'll get old waiting for that.'

Straightening up to his full commanding height, Bastien strolled forward, fluid as a predator tracking prey. 'Don't keep me in suspense. Option two? Or option three?'

'*Three*… Although I should warn you, you've picked the wrong woman.'

'Three…' Bastien's accent made a three-course meal of the word as he savoured it with immense satisfaction. 'In what way are you the wrong woman?'

Lilah shifted uneasily from one foot to the other. 'I haven't got the experience you'll probably expect,' she told him stiffly, deeply disturbed by his increasing closeness and fighting the revealing urge to step back out of reach.

'I've got enough experience for both of us,' Bastien purred, dark eyes flashing gold as he stared down at her. 'Are you trying to tell me that you haven't indulged that side of your nature very often?'

'Haven't indulged it at all,' she countered curtly, lifting her chin, standing her ground, refusing to feel embarrassed. 'I'm a virgin.'

Bastien actually backed away a couple of feet, his lean chiselled features setting into rigid angles of shock while his eyes flared more golden than ever below the thick canopy of his black lashes. 'Is that a tease?'

Lilah gave him a grim glance. 'No, it's not. I just thought I should warn you in case it's a deal-breaker.'

'Are you telling me the truth?' Bastien prompted in a roughened undertone, prowling closer again and circling her like a stalking panther. 'You're a *virgin*?'

Colour ran up below her pale cheeks but she held his fierce gaze. 'Yes.'

'If you're telling me the truth it's not a deal-breaker—it's the biggest turn-on I've ever had,' Bastien confessed, thoroughly shocking her with that assurance.

Bastien was disturbingly conscious that for once he was not uttering a mere soundbite for effect. He had never been with a virgin. When he was a teenager his partners had all been older, and when the age range of his lovers had begun to match his own maturity he had never dallied or even *wanted* to dally with a sexually innocent woman. For a start, he had never been attracted to young, immature girls. In addition he did very much like sex, and he had no time for those who would stick limits on a physical outlet he saw as both natural and free.

Yet something strange was happening to his views

while he looked at Delilah, because he was discovering that when those same limits were applied to her and her innocence he was happy with the idea…and even happier at the prospect of becoming her first lover. He didn't understand why he felt that way, because he had never been a possessive man, and nor had he ever been remotely unsure of his own skills in the bedroom and afraid of comparison.

A frown settled between his brows while he attempted to penetrate the mystery of his own gratification at her announcement—until the obvious answer came to him. What he found appealing had to be the sheer novelty of the experience she offered him…*of course* she would be something different, something new, something fresh!

'That's disgusting,' Lilah told him furiously. 'How can you admit something like that?'

Uncomfortably aroused by his thoughts, Bastien wanted to reach for her and demonstrate exactly how he felt, but he knew it wasn't the right moment. The nervous flicker of her bright blue eyes, her very restiveness, warned him that if he gave her sufficient ammunition she would take off in a panic like a hare bolting for its burrow.

'I will want you to sign a confidentiality agreement,' he told her levelly, sticking strictly to practicality. 'That's standard. It means that you will never be able to talk about our association in public or in private.'

Her nose wrinkled with distaste. 'I hardly think I would *want* to talk about it,' she said drily, fighting the nerves leaping in her stomach.

'In return I will purchase a suitable house for your father and his family.'

Lilah squared her slight shoulders. 'No, you will not. I don't want my family to be suspicious about my supposed job with you, and if you splash around too much cash they will definitely be suspicious. Give my father employment and he'll take care of his own family without any further help from *you*,' she told him with quiet pride.

'I'll want you to fly down to London with me tomorrow.'

Her eyes flew wide. *'Tomorrow?'*

'I'll call your father in to see me today and share the good news. I'll inform him that you're joining my personal staff. You can go home early to pack and you can dine with me at my hotel tonight.'

'I have a prior arrangement to meet friends.'

'To do what?' Bastien demanded impatiently.

'To eat out and see a movie.'

Bastien compressed his wide, sensual mouth. He wanted to tell her that in the near future she would do nothing without his permission. It was astonishing how much pleasure that belief gave him. But he didn't need to crack the whip right here and now, did he? She would be his soon enough and he would share her with no one—not friends, not family, no one.

Was that what could be described as a 'possessive' thought? His skin chilled at the suspicion. No, the thought was born of the reality that he had had to wait so long for Delilah that he wanted and indeed expected to receive one hundred per cent of her attention. He was not and never would be a possessive man, he assured himself with confidence. Even so, now that Delilah was officially set to become part of his life, in a way no other woman had ever been, he would ensure that she was protected by telling one of his security team to keep an eye on her from a discreet distance.

Lilah watched as Bastien unfurled his cell phone, stabbed out a number and spoke at length in Greek—short, staccato phrases that sounded very much like instructions.

'My driver will take you home now,' he informed her smoothly. 'And wait to collect your father and bring him back here to see me.'

Lilah hovered, because he made it all seem so bloodless and impersonal. Nothing she had said had changed his outlook about what he was doing. He neither regretted nor questioned his callous methods. He wanted her and he didn't care what he had to do to get her. The passion that had to power such an unapologetic desire for her body shook Lilah.

He closed a hand round hers and entrapped her without warning. 'Evidently I won't see you now until tomorrow, when we meet on my plane. It's probably just as well that you're seeing friends tonight. It takes the focus off us,' he pointed out with grudging appreciation. 'It will be more comfortable for all of us that way.'

'Certainly for you…if it keeps my father in the dark,' Lilah gibed.

'Do you honestly think I care about his opinion?' Bastien countered thickly. 'We're single adults. What we do in private is our business.'

Long dark fingers closed round her other hand, tugging her closer, fully entrapping her.

'Our business alone,' Bastien repeated thickly, lowering his arrogant dark head to hers and teasing along the tense line of her full lower lip with the blunt edge of his teeth, before soothing it with his tongue in a provocative caress that caught her unprepared and sent liquid heat to pool in her pelvis.

'We're at *work*, for goodness' sake!' Lilah protested in a rattled undertone.

'It's just a kiss,' Bastien husked, delving between her parted lips with his tongue and plunging deep with an unashamed hunger that roared through her like a bush fire.

Her knees locked and her legs swayed and she grabbed his forearms to steady herself, fingers clenching into the fabric of his suit jacket in consternation.

Just a kiss.

A little voice reminded her that in the near future she would have to give him a great deal more than a kiss. His mouth hardened on hers, hot and demanding, and a sensation like an electric shock tingled through her, awakening her body as nothing else had ever done. Her nipples pinched into tight buds of sensitivity; the secret flesh between her legs pulsed with sudden dampness. It was a wanting—a fierce wanting unlike anything she had ever felt before—and she was appalled by the response he was wringing from her treacherous body.

A lean hand clamped her spine to force her closer, and against her stomach she felt the hard swell of his erection even through the barrier of their clothing. A surge of burning heat that was very far from revulsion engulfed her and her face burned even hotter as he set her back from him with controlled force.

'I shouldn't start something I can't finish,' Bastien quipped.

Desperately flailing for something…*anything*…to distract her from the attack of self-loathing waiting to pounce on her, Lilah paused on her way to the door. 'Is it all right if I bring my dog with me tomorrow?'

'No pets. Leave the dog with your family.'

'I can't. My stepmother isn't comfortable with dogs. He's very small and quiet,' Lilah assured Bastien, lying through her teeth because Skippy wasn't remotely quiet once he got to know people.

Bastien frowned. 'Write down its details. I'll arrange for a specialist transport firm to handle the travel arrangements,' he pronounced after a considered pause. 'But once the animal arrives in France keep it away from me.'

'France?' she repeated in consternation.

'We're going to France the day after tomorrow.'

Lilah tottered back downstairs, shattered by the way she had succumbed to that single kiss. How could Bastien still have that effect on her? She hadn't been prepared for that. Perhaps naively she had assumed that her disgust at the unholy agreement he had offered her would protect her. But it hadn't.

Bastien had bought her acquiescence with a job for her father and the promised long-term prosperity of the reopened factory. Didn't he see how wrong that deal was? That reducing her body to the level of something to be traded like a product made her hate him? Didn't that matter to him?

But why should it matter to him? she questioned heavily as she informed Julie that she was leaving early. Bastien only wanted sex. He wasn't interested in what went on inside her head or how she felt about him. He didn't care… And neither should *she* care, she told herself defiantly. Being oversensitive in Bastien's radius was only going to get her hurt and humiliated. He wouldn't give her the kind of polite or gracious pretences that would allow her to save face. There would be no frills in the way of romance or compliments. He wasn't about to dress up their connection by making it about anything more than sex.

Later that same evening, in the wake of a whirlwind of embarrassingly untruthful explanations on the home front and a great deal of packing, Lilah emerged from the cinema with Josh—a tall, attractive man in his twenties, with brown hair and green eyes—and two other couples, Ann and Jack and Dana and George. There was nothing like a good fright or two to dispel tension, Lilah acknowledged wryly as she laughed at something Ann said about the horror movie they had watched.

'You're making a wise move on the career front,' Josh told her. 'Doing HR at Moore wasn't stretching you. Working for an international businessman will offer you much more experience.'

A shamefaced flush lit Lilah's face, because her friends had swallowed her lies about going to work for Bastien hook, line and sinker—just as her family had. 'I suppose so…'

'Very bad timing for me, though.' Without warning Josh reached for both her hands. 'You're leaving just when I was about to ask you out on a *real* date.'

'What?' Lilah's voice was shrill with surprise.

Josh grinned down at her, ignoring Jack's mocking wolf whistle. 'I mean, you must have wondered at least once what it would be like if we got together.'

Lilah grimaced, not knowing what to say to him. Because she never *had* wondered.

Josh edged her back against the wall behind her. 'Just one kiss,' he muttered.

Lilah stiffened, wondering why she felt like a stick of rock with 'Property of Bastien Zikos' stamped all the way through her. 'No, Josh,' she said, her hands braced against his chest.

But because she couldn't bring herself to actively push him away he kissed her, and she felt much as a shop window mannequin might have felt…absolutely nothing. Because while she liked Josh, and enjoyed his company, she had never fancied him.

'While you're away think about the possibility of *us*,' Josh urged, stretching an arm round her to guide her towards his parked car.

'I don't think so,' Lilah responded, wondering if there was a kind way of telling a man that you didn't fancy him in the slightest and knowing that there wasn't, and that the best response was probably for her just to pretend that absolutely nothing had happened.

'Awkward…' Ann mouthed, her eyes rolling with sympathy.

When Lilah walked back into her living room she was surprised by the expression of sincere happiness on her father's face. But she knew that even before she had reached home that afternoon Bastien had phoned her father, and the older man had already put on a suit by the time the car bringing his daughter home had arrived. When Lilah had gone out to meet her friends her father had still been out, presumably still with Bastien, which had worried Lilah.

'Everything all right, Dad?' she questioned anxiously.

'Better than that,' the older man assured her with vigour, and informed her that Bastien had hired him to act as manager at Moore Components—a role which he was very happy to take on.

'I'm beginning to understand how Bastien has become so very rich so fast,' the older man remarked in wry addition. 'He's very astute, and he spotted a break that would benefit Moore when no one else did.'

'What? *What* did he spot?' Lilah prompted with a frown.

'Bastien recognised that the council has recently rezoned the town's plans to open the door for further development. He's selling the current site for a *huge* amount of money and relocating the factory to the Moat Road, where he'll qualify for all sorts of lucrative government grants when he reopens for business. It's an incredibly smart move.'

'Good grief!' Lilah gasped, shock and temper bubbling up inside her at the belated awareness that Bastien had cut a very good deal with her in *every* way. Not only was he getting *her*, parcelled up like a gift, but he was also evidently on course to make a big profit too! And that realisation absolutely enraged Lilah.

CHAPTER FOUR

LILAH BOARDED BASTIEN'S private jet with her head held
high. No, she wasn't about to show the shame she felt,
and she wasn't anyone's victim—least of all Bastien's.
This was *her* choice, she reminded herself doggedly.
Bastien might have laid out those hateful options but
she had made the choice, and she was still happy with
what her sacrifice had achieved for her family.

Her father was managing the business he loved.
For the moment he and Vickie would stay on in Lilah's little house, because it was affordable and within
easy reach of Ben's school. Lilah thought her father
and stepmother probably couldn't quite credit that life
had changed for the better again. Having so recently
lost everything, they were afraid of another disaster.

Lilah had had tears in her eyes when she'd parted
from her little brother and sister that morning, for she
had no idea when she would see them again. Did a
mistress get time off from her role? Would she have
any rights at all?

Bastien rested his arrogant dark head back to survey
Delilah as she walked into the cabin. His mouth took
on a sardonic curve when he saw her. She wore a

drab, dated black trouser suit and had braided her hair again, concealing her every attraction to the best of her ability. But Bastien was hard to fool. She couldn't conceal the supple elegance of her delicate build or the healthy youthful glow of her fair skin and bright blue eyes, and when the jacket of her suit flapped back, revealing a sheer white shirt that hugged her small pouting breasts like a second skin, the fit of his trousers became uncomfortably tight.

Tonight, he thought impatiently, would finally rid him of the almost adolescent state of arousal she inflicted on him. A virgin, though… Was that really the truth? Didn't that deserve a certain amount of considerate staging?

Since when had he been considerate? Bastien asked himself irritably as Delilah attempted to walk past him towards the back of the cabin, where his staff were seated. His hand snapped out to close round her wrist and bring her to a halt.

'You sit with me,' he told her flatly.

Her full pink mouth tightened.

'Take off that ugly jacket. Let down your hair,' Bastien instructed.

Lilah froze. 'What will you do if I say no?'

'Rip off the jacket and yank out the hair tie for you,' Bastien traded without hesitation.

Warm colour flooded Lilah's cheeks and feathery lashes lowered over her eyes, because she was insanely conscious of his staff watching from the other end of the cabin. They were clearly wondering what she was doing on board and were now about to have their curiosity satisfied. She shrugged out of the jacket stiffly and reached up to tug at the tie anchoring her braid. Her hand was shaking as she loosened her hair.

Rage and mortification gusted through her as she dropped down into the seat beside Bastien, glossy black curls fanning in tousled disarray across her shoulders and brushing her flushed cheekbones.

'And just like that you look gorgeous again, *koukla mou*.'

'Is it going to be like this with everything? Your way or the highway?' Lilah pressed in a strangled hiss.

'What do *you* think?'

'That I once thought you were enough of a man not to need to control a woman's every move!'

His lean, darkly handsome features slashed into a sudden, entirely unexpected grin, his pride untouched by that crack. 'The trouble is…I *enjoy* controlling you.'

Lilah snatched in a much-needed gulp of oxygen. He sent her temper zooming from zero to sixty in the space of seconds. She had never considered herself quick-tempered until she met Bastien, but he literally set her teeth on edge almost every time he spoke.

'Why would you even want a woman who doesn't want you? Or is that what it takes to turn you on?'

That was a suggestion that deeply affronted Bastien, for the merest hint of aversion to him from a lover would have repulsed him.

He turned round to face her more directly, his dark eyes flaming gold as ingots, and closed a hand into the fall of her hair to hold her still. 'No, *you're* what it takes to turn me on…but, believe me, you can make very angry.'

'Is that a fact?' Lilah whispered tauntingly, tilting her chin, blue eyes gleaming.

In a searing movement of sensual intimidation Bastien crushed her soft mouth under his, driving her lips apart for the stabbing penetration of his tongue. She wasn't able to breathe, but then at that moment she didn't *want* to breathe. Her head was swimming, her body stinging with wild awareness, and a roaring hunger was awakening like a hurricane deep down inside her.

For a count of ten energising seconds Bastien thought about carrying her into the sleeping compartment and sating himself on her. But he would hurt her. He knew he was too hyped up for control. Besides, it was only a short flight to London and the jet would be landing soon.

He pulled back from her, positively aching from the throbbing force of his desire. 'You *do* want me,' he contradicted thickly, scanning her wildly flushed face and swollen, reddened mouth with satisfaction. 'You did from the first, *koukla mou.*'

Lilah whipped her attention away from him again and stared into space. *Well, you asked for that,* she told herself crossly, wondering why she always felt such a driving need to try to shoot Bastien down in flames. Unfortunately, in spite of all her efforts to ground him, he kept on soaring heavenward like a rocket.

Even so she was being confronted by a truth that she couldn't bear to examine. From the very first glimpse she had got of Bastien she *had* wanted him, and the hunger he had awakened in her was both primitive and terrifying. It truly hadn't mattered who he was or even what he was like, because her body had instantly seethed with a life of its own, wanting to connect with his, and her brain had swum with new and disturbing erotic images.

She hadn't known attraction could be that immediate or that powerful, and had certainly never suspected that it could overwhelm all restraint and common sense. Even worse, she was painfully aware that, had Bastien employed a more subtle approach and less honesty, he most probably would have succeeded in seducing her into his bed.

The cabin crew served drinks, the glamorous blonde stewardess syrupy sweet and persistent in her determination to serve and flirt with Bastien at the same time. He ignored her behaviour as if it wasn't happening, neither looking directly at the woman nor responding to her inviting chatter.

'Where are we going?' Lilah asked once the jet had landed.

'I'm taking you shopping, and tomorrow we head to Paris. I have a business meeting there.'

'Shopping?' she queried in surprise.

Bastien shrugged a broad shoulder and said nothing. Lilah caught the stewardess studying her with naked envy and thought, *If only you knew the truth.*

But what *was* the real truth? Lilah asked herself as the limo whisked her and Bastien through the crowded streets of London. She had given her word and Bastien had already delivered on his promises, which meant that he owned her body and soul for the foreseeable future. And that interpretation cast her as a complete victim, Lilah acknowledged ruefully—until she admitted the reality that one glance at Bastien's exquisitely chiselled features and tall athletic physique reduced her to a melted puddle of lust and longing. He was incredibly attractive—and, taking into account his reputation as a legendary womaniser, a very large number of women agreed with her.

They were met at the door of a world-famous store and conveyed upwards in a lift, surrounded by a posse of attendants composed of a stylist, a personal shopper and sales assistants. Clearly Bastien had already stated his preferences, and they were shown into a private room where he was ushered into a seat. Lilah hovered, watching the approach of a tray of champagne, and then she was steered into a changing room, where an astonishingly large selection of clothing awaited her.

Surely trying on loads of clothes for Bastien's benefit wasn't the *worst* thing that could have happened to her? But if making her model the clothes he wanted her to wear was a deliberate ploy to annoy her, he had played a blinder. The demeaning concept of swanning around in clothing personally picked by Bastien set her teeth on edge.

With a flush on her cheeks, she stepped back into the room clad in a blue silk dress that clung to her like cling film.

Bastien kicked back in his comfortable chair, very much in the mood to enjoy himself. His burnished gaze rested on Delilah and the oddest sense of contentment settled over him. Amusement tilted his handsome mouth when she teetered dangerously in the very high heels she clearly wasn't accustomed to walking in. The dress was rubbish: far too revealing. The only place Delilah would be encouraged to show that amount of flesh was in his bedroom and nowhere else.

He moved a dismissive hand and awaited the next

outfit, a pale pink jacket and skirt that was cute as hell against her cloud of blue-black hair and bright blue eyes. There might not be much of her, Bastien conceded, but what she lacked in curves she more than made up for in class, and with a delicacy that he considered incredibly feminine. The first time he had seen Delilah she had put him in mind of a flawless porcelain doll—until he'd noticed how expressive her face was: an ever-changing fascinating vista of what she was feeling and thinking. And what he liked most about her face was that he could read it as easily as a child's picture book.

'I'm not modelling underwear for you,' she warned him in a biting undertone.

Disconcerted, Bastien froze and lifted his arrogant, dark head to meet her bright eyes head-on, finally recognising the blaze of anger banked down there. 'Not a problem,' he assured her lazily. 'We'll save that show for the bedroom, *glikia mou*.'

Lilah's cheeks blazed with sudden livid colour. 'No, that's not me,' she parried abruptly. 'If that's what you want, you've picked the wrong girl!'

'You're perfect for me,' Bastien assured her levelly.

'Well, that's not a compliment I can return,' Lilah replied tartly. 'After all, it's obvious that we're a match made in hell. You want a dress-up doll that does exactly what's it's told and I won't do that.'

Bastien rose lithely to his feet and looked down at her from his commanding height with unreadable dark eyes. 'That's not what I want.'

'You want all the imperfections airbrushed away. You want obedience. Clearly you want a woman with submissive traits, and yet I don't have a submissive bone in my body! In fact, I'm more likely to *argue* with people who make unreasonable demands,' Lilah shot back at him in angry frustration. 'You're the king of unreasonable demands, Bastien. So, what are you doing with *me*?'

'You're misinterpreting everything I've ever said to you,' Bastien told her drily.

'Am I?' Lilah rolled her bright blue eyes, unimpressed by that accusation. 'You're such a control freak that you even want to choose the clothes I wear.'

'That's untrue,' Bastien incised. 'You're more like a jewel I want to see polished up and placed in the right setting. I don't want to see you wearing cheap clothes... I want to see you shine—'

'Bastien!' Lilah broke in helplessly, hopelessly confused by his attitude. He only wanted to have sex with her. He had been brutally honest about that reality. What did the clothes she wore have to do with a hunger that basic? Why on earth did he care what she wore?

She had paraded around for his benefit in one outfit after another. A vast wardrobe was being assembled for her use. She was stunned by that reality as well. For goodness' sake, was Bastien planning to keep her for the rest of her life—and his? How would she ever wear even a quarter of these clothes while she was with him? This was a male who was famed for barely lasting a month with one woman. Yet she had been equipped with countless wardrobe choices— indeed, everything a woman could conceivably want for every possible occasion and every season. Late afternoon had already stretched well into evening to encompass the shopping trip.

'We'll go back to the hotel now for dinner,' Bastien proposed, as if no dispute had taken place.

Lilah returned to the changing cubicle and selected a skirt and top from the rack to put on. She was being torn in two. On one level she wanted to fight Bastien, but on another she wanted to give him what he wanted to keep him happy. After all, how much was her own pride really worth when she could still clearly recall her father's renewed energy and hope?

What Bastien had given could easily be taken away again, she reflected fearfully. By giving her father a job, Bastien had revitalised the older man's drive and confidence. She should be grateful, she told herself urgently, but it was no use—she was too idealistic for such practicality. Unlike Bastien, she wanted sex to come packaged with romance and commitment.

Bastien took her back to an exclusive hotel and a very spacious suite. There were two bedrooms, and in the doorway of the first, Bastien paused to say, 'This is your room. I like my own space.'

Relieved by the news that she would not have to share a bedroom and surrender *all* privacy, Lilah watched as the hotel staff carted in the boxes and bags containing her brand-new wardrobe as well as a sizeable collection of designer luggage.

Bastien turned to grasp the phone extended to him by one of his personal assistants. Lean, strong face intent, he began talking urgently in French while raising an impatient hand to summon his team. As he spoke he strode to the desk in the large reception room, where a laptop had already been set up for his use.

His attention had drifted away from Lilah at supersonic speed. She watched his staff move into action, unfurling phones and tablets to follow Bastien's instructions. One name was mentioned repeatedly—Dufort Pharmaceuticals.

She kicked off her high heels and switched on the television in the far corner of the room. The fancy evening meal she had expected to eat in Bastien's company did not materialise. Instead, about an hour later waiters arrived with trolleys of buffet food to feed staff more interested in standing upright to eat than sitting down.

'Delilah!' Bastien called across the length of the room. 'Eat…you must be hungry by now.'

'Starving,' she admitted, padding over to him barefoot to grasp the plate he extended, daunted by the sheer size of him when she stood next to him without her shoes.

'A promising business deal has come up,' Bastien confided, studying her casually tousled hair and teeny-tiny bare toes, admiring the lack of vanity that allowed her to relax to that extent in his presence. She didn't care about impressing him, and he respected her innate sense of self-worth.

'I guessed that…' Lilah hid her amusement, delighted not to be the sole focus of his attention.

Ebony brows pleating, Bastien watched Delilah curl up on the sofa to return to the reality show she was watching. She was simply accepting that business came first for him without either taking offence or angling for a greater share of his attention. Yet, watching her relax back into the sofa and start eating with appetite, Bastien wondered if *he* should be the one taking offence—because it really wasn't a compliment that she should be so unconcerned by his preoccupation.

Becoming bored after an hour, Delilah switched off the television and crammed her feet back into the shoes she had kicked off to stand up. It was too early for bed and she was restless.

'Where are you going?' Bastien asked as she moved towards the door.

'For a walk. I need a break.'

Delilah was stepping into the lift when, to her surprise, one of Bastien's security team joined her.

'Is Bastien scared I'm going to run away?' she gasped in frustration, recognising the young man.

'I'm afraid you're stuck with me.' Her companion sighed. 'My instructions are not to let you out of my sight.'

'What's your name?' she asked.

'Ciro.'

'I'm Lilah,' she responded with a rueful smile, knowing that it wasn't fair to take her irritation out on Ciro, who was only guilty of doing his job.

A pianist was playing in the low-lit bar on the ground floor. Sitting down, Lilah ordered a drink. Ciro retreated to a table by the wall and left her in peace. Wishing she had thought to tuck a book into her bag, Lilah decided to catch up on her phone calls instead.

She rang her father first. Robert Moore talked non-stop to his daughter about Bastien's plans for the business and the advantages of the new location Bastien had picked for the firm. Lilah followed up that call with one to Vickie, learning that her dog, Skippy, had been picked up on schedule by a transport firm that morning.

She was replacing her phone in her bag when a

blonde woman sat down without warning in the seat opposite her. Lilah looked up in disconcertion.

'You're staying here with Bastien Zikos, aren't you?' the woman pressed with a smile.

Lilah's brows pleated. 'Why are you asking me that?'

'I'm Jenny Gower and I write for the women's page on the *Daily Pageant*,' the blonde told Lilah cheerfully, setting a business card down in front of her. 'That's my number. Feel free to call me any time you'd like a chat. Bastien's a real favourite with our readers and we like to keep up to date with his latest ladies.'

The woman was a reporter, Lilah realised in dismay. 'I've got nothing to say to you,' she said uncomfortably.

'Don't be shy. We pay generously for even little titbits.'

Without warning Ciro appeared at her elbow and intervened. 'Lilah…you're talking to a journalist.'

Lilah stiffened. 'We're not actually talking. I was just about to leave.'

And with that last word Lilah finished her drink and left the table.

'Mr Zikos loathes gossip columnists,' Ciro warned her with a grimace. 'I'll try to avoid mentioning the fact that you were approached.'

When Lilah returned to the suite Bastien was in the act of dismissing his staff for the night. 'I was planning to come down and join you,' he informed her.

Lilah flinched and coloured, focusing on Bastien with her heart in her mouth.

Annoyance flared in Bastien when he recognised the apprehension flashing in her gaze. Women didn't shrink from him; they *wanted* him. She must've been telling the truth about her inexperience, he concluded grimly. Only ignorance could explain such an attitude. It was surely past time that he showed her that she had nothing to fear from him.

'Would you like a drink?' he asked lazily, strolling closer.

'No, thanks,' she said jerkily.

Bastien crossed the room and scooped her right off her feet. Loosing a startled gasp, she wriggled like an electrified eel, strands of coconut-scented hair brushing his cheek as she moved her head back and forth.

'Relax,' he urged.

'Are you *kidding*?' Lilah exclaimed.

'You said you were a virgin. You didn't tell me that you were a hysterical one,' Bastien derided.

Lilah froze in his arms as though she had been slapped. She *was* overreacting, she acknowledged ruefully. Obviously Bastien was going to touch her, so his move shouldn't have sent her into panic mode.

'I'm *not* hysterical,' she protested, dry mouthed.

'You could've fooled me,' Bastien traded, settling down in an armchair with her slim body still firmly clasped to his broad chest.

'You startled me…you *pounced*,' Lilah condemned.

'And I'm not about to apologise for it,' Bastien husked, running down the back zip on her top and tugging it off her arms in one smooth movement.

'Oh…' Lilah gasped again, shocked to find herself stripped down to her bra without ceremony.

Bastien splayed a big hand across her narrow midriff to hold her in place while his mouth moved urgently across the pale skin at the nape of her neck.

Her heart hammered inside her tight chest and a tiny uncontrollable shiver racked her when his teeth grazed and nipped along the slope between her neck and her shoulder. It was a fiercely erotic assault, subsequently soothed by the skim of his tongue.

Her eyes flew wide, her pupils expanding as quiver after quiver of response gripped her. Suddenly even breathing became a challenge. Bastien closed his hands to her waist to lift her and turn her to face him, bringing her down again with her skirt hitched and her legs splayed either side of his hips.

His tongue plunged against hers in a deep, marauding kiss that made her tremble. Her bra felt too tight and the ache stirring in her pelvis was powerful enough to hurt. He kept on kissing her, forcing her lips apart with urgency and drawing her down on him so that she could feel the hard thrust of his erection between her spread thighs.

'Bastien... I—'

Dark golden eyes accentuated by a canopy of black velvet lashes held hers and silenced her. He truly had the most stunning eyes. Her mouth ran dry. Her mind was as blank as an unpainted canvas because she was reeling from the intensity of what he was making her feel.

She didn't even realise he had flicked loose her bra until he ran his hands up over her pert breasts to make actual skin-to-skin contact. Her usual alarm about her lack of size in the breast department had no time to develop, because his hands were already curving to the small pale mounds. With knowing fingers and thumbs he roughly tugged and chafed the pale pink sensitivity of her straining nipples. His touch sent hot tingles of longing arrowing through her limp body, heat and moisture gathering at the pulsing heart of her.

'You have such pretty breasts,' Bastien said thickly, bending her back over his supporting arm to capture a swollen stiff bud between his lips and torment it with attention. 'And so very sensitive, *koukla mou...*'

Her breath see-sawed back and forth in her throat while he rocked her over his lean, powerful body, ensuring that on every downward motion her tender core connected with the hard swell of his arousal. The tightening sensation in her womb increased to an unbearable level. Long fingers skated over the taut fabric stretched between her legs, where she was excruciatingly sensitive. He eased a finger below the lace edge of her panties. Excitement roared through her as he stroked and rubbed the tender bud of her clitoris. Rational thought vanished, because her body was greedily craving every new sensation, living from one intoxicating moment to the next.

As he rimmed the tiny wet entrance to her body with a teasing fingertip and at the same time let his carnal mouth latch hungrily on to an agonisingly tender nipple, Lilah's every nerve ending went into screaming overdrive.

'Come for me, Delilah,' Bastien told her rawly.

And then there was no holding back the explosion of excitement that had risen to a high Lilah could no longer suppress. Within seconds she was crying out, shuddering and convulsing with the wild surge of pleasure Bastien's expert hands had released. Exhausted and drained in the aftermath, she let her head drop down against his shoulder, barely able to credit that her body could react so powerfully that it still felt as though she was coming apart at the seams. He smelt of expensive cologne, testosterone and clean musky male, and at that moment—astonishingly—it was the most comforting scent she had ever experienced.

The strangest sense of protectiveness crept through Bastien while Delilah clung to him. He licked his fingers, her unique taste adding another layer to his fierce arousal. He wanted more—so much more that he knew he dared not let himself touch her again until he had cooled down. Unfortunately he had never been a patient man, and he knew his own faults.

He stood up, cradling her slight body in his arms, and carried her through to her room, where he settled her down on the bed.

'I'll see you in the morning.'

Conscious of the cool air hitting her bare breasts, Lilah crossed her arms across her body with a defensive jerk and looked up at Bastien in astonishment as he switched on the bedside lamp. That was it? He wasn't joining her in the bed to finish what he had started?

Hot colour surged in her cheeks as she collided with glittering dark golden eyes. 'But...'

'Tonight was for you, not for me,' Bastien told her wryly, striding back to the door and then coming to a halt to glance back at her with a blindingly charismatic smile that mesmerised her into staring. 'You know the weirdest thing...?'

His lean, darkly handsome features were pure fallen angel in the shadowy light. 'No...' she whispered, almost hypnotised by the flawless perfection of his sculpted features.

'What we just did...' he mused, with a self-mocking

curve to his beautiful mouth. 'That has to be the most innocent experience I've ever shared with a woman.'

As the door thudded shut on his exit Lilah's brows lifted almost as high as her hairline. *Innocent?* How could such shattering intimacy be in any way innocent? What on earth was he talking about?

Her body was still aching and quaking as though it had come through a battle zone. She slid off the bed and staggered dizzily into the en-suite bathroom, challenged to place even one foot accurately in front of the other. There she studied her tousled reflection in disgust. Her hair was messy, her mascara smeared and she was half-naked.

With a groan of shame she stripped off the skirt and panties and stepped into the shower. But even beneath the cleansing, cooling flow of water her body tingled and burned with new awareness in the places Bastien had touched.

Lilah shuddered—and *not* in disgust—at the thought of him doing it again. That acknowledgement alone was sufficient to keep her tossing and turning half the night.

CHAPTER FIVE

'COULD I HAVE a quiet word, sir?'

Manos, Bastien's head of security, approached him as he was still working, close to midnight. The older man seemed uncomfortable.

'It relates to Miss Moore...'

And within the space of minutes Bastien's even-tempered mood had been destroyed by the information Manos put in front of him.

Having initially assumed that Delilah was simply another employee, Manos had only belatedly realised that the news that she had been seen consorting with another man might be of interest to Bastien.

Bastien was shocked. And then furious with himself for *being* shocked. After all, how many times had a woman let him down? Lied to him? Ripped him off? Faked emotions to impress him? Too many times to count, Bastien conceded, tight mouthed with cynicism, his lean, starkly handsome bone structure rigid. But as far as he was aware not a single one of his lovers had ever *cheated* on him.

Forewarned is forearmed, Bastien told himself forbiddingly. And if Delilah had been with another man as recently as the night before, he no longer wanted her, did he? Damn Security for not following her home to establish exactly how the evening had concluded!

Frustration building at this incomplete picture of events, Bastien clenched his fists, plunged upright and decided to go out. The frustration was fast becoming rage, in a vicious tide that came with a bitter backwash.

A virgin? Of *course* Delilah was not a virgin! How likely had that claim ever been? Obviously she had made up that story in an effort to make him feel guilty while she played the poor little victim. And he didn't do victims any more than he did relationships, did he? Delilah Moore was toxic for him. Hadn't he suspected as much two years earlier? When had he ever wanted one particular woman that much? Any hunger that particular wasn't healthy.

Bastien headed for an exclusive nightclub to find another woman for the night. He had to prove to his own satisfaction that he was not remotely concerned by what he had learned about Delilah. She was not special in any way, he told himself furiously, downing his third drink in fast succession. She was like every other woman he had ever met: immediately... *easily*...replaceable.

In the club, Bastien was surrounded by beautiful women eager to attract his attention. He waited for one to give him a buzz, studying a blonde and deciding she was too voluptuous. A brunette who had eyes that were too close together. A redhead who laughed like a hyena. Another wore a hideous floral dress, and yet another had enormous feet.

Delilah's were the very first female feet Bastien had ever actually noticed, he acknowledged abstractedly. She had very small feet, with teeny-tiny toes and nails like polished pearls.

He settled into his fourth drink and wondered first of all why he was thinking about feet and then why he was still on his own. Why the hell was he suddenly being so fastidious? *Any* attractive woman would do. Hadn't he always believed that? He did not, *could* not, still want a woman who had cheated on him.

So what was he planning to do about Delilah?

Bastien registered that he wanted to confront her, and that strange urge deeply unsettled him. After all, he had always avoided high drama, and he had never, ever argued with the women who'd shared his bed. Why would he argue when women who annoyed him were instantly banished from his life, never to hear from him again?

He would send Delilah back up north, forget about her, cut his losses....

When the bedroom door opened abruptly Lilah was jolted awake. She sat up. Light was flooding the doorway to silhouette a powerful male figure. Instantly she knew it was Bastien, and instantly she was apprehensive.

The light was snapped on, momentarily blinding her, and Bastien strode in. His lean bronzed features were clenched ferociously hard, and his eyes, dark as eternal night, glittered above high lancing cheekbones. Her tummy performed a nervous dance and she backed up against the pillows with her knees defensively raised.

'I want a word with you.'

Bastien sent the door behind him thudding shut and her throat closed over convulsively.

A faint whiff of alcohol assailed her nose; he had been drinking. For the first time Lilah was appreciating that she knew very little about Bastien Zikos—basically only what she had read on the internet, none of which was reassuring. Did he drink a lot? Was he drunk now? Was he violent? Was such random temperamental behaviour the norm for him?

'Stop looking at me like that…' Bastien growled in frowning reproof, studying her from below the thick canopy of his black lashes.

Clutching the duvet to her with a nervous hand, Lilah breathed out. 'Like what?'

'As if you're scared!' Bastien grated accusingly. 'I have never hurt a woman in my life.'

A tentative half smile stole some of the tension from Lilah's triangular face. 'You just walked in… You startled me… I was fast asleep,' she explained, struggling to excuse herself rather than tell him the truth.

And the truth was that Bastien *was* scary. He was very tall, very muscular, much larger and stronger than she was in every way. Moreover, although he had the hauntingly beautiful face of a fallen angel, his dark eyes currently had a piercing, chilling light that utterly intimidated her.

'I want you to tell me where you were and who you were with last night,' Bastien bit out harshly, taking up a brooding stance at the very foot of the bed. 'Don't leave anything out.'

'I was out with a group of friends,' Lilah almost whispered, wondering why on earth he could be demanding such an explanation. 'We went for a meal and then to the cinema.'

'Do you normally kiss your male friends and then climb into a car to go home with them at the end of the night?' Bastien asked grimly.

Her eyes widened and flickered in dismay, colour warming her pale face. 'How do you know there was a kiss?'

Bastien was watching her face, recognising the embarrassment and the sudden flash of resentment there but seeing not a shred of guilt. 'I had one of my security team watching you last night. He lost track of you after you got into the guy's car.'

'Oh…' It was the only thing Lilah could initially think to say, because she was hugely disconcerted by the idea that someone Bastien employed had been following her round before she'd even left her home town. How dared he invade her privacy like that? 'You had no right to have anyone watching me.'

'From the moment I let you into my life I had that right. Did you spend the night with him?'

Battling to keep her temper over that far-reaching declaration of his rights over her, Lilah swallowed hard. 'No, I didn't. Josh dropped me straight home. There was one kiss, Bastien, nothing more.' She frowned at him, dismayed by the depth of his distrust. 'He's never kissed me before, and I wasn't expecting it. He was just trying it on.'

'You didn't try to stop him.'

'He's a friend and we had an audience.' Lilah grimaced. 'I didn't want to make a big scene of rejecting him in front of everyone. It would have made us all feel horribly uncomfortable.'

Bastien studied her, torn between belief and disbelief. His lean, strong features remained hard and set, his tawny eyes veiled by his lashes. The silence lay there, thick as a swamp between them.

'You were too generous. You're mine now,' Bastien told her in a raw, gritty undertone. 'I will not tolerate any other man touching you.'

'Bastien…I don't want anyone following me around, spying on me.'

'It goes with the territory. It's for my peace of mind and your protection.'

'I don't need protection.'

'That's my decision,' Bastien decreed, snapping off the light in a sudden movement that made her flinch.

'Bastien…?' Lilah whispered.

A powerful silhouette, he hovered. 'What?'

'Sometimes you really, really annoy me.'

'That cuts both ways.'

Bastien studied her slight figure in the bed and then strode into the room to flip back the duvet and scoop her up into his arms.

'What are you doing?' she gasped in consternation as he strode into the room next door to hers.

Bastien thrust back the sheet on his bed and settled her on the mattress. 'I want you where I can see you,' he told her curtly.

'You told me that I was getting my own room,' she reminded him breathlessly.

'For what remains of tonight, I've changed my mind.' Removing his jacket, he cast it on a chair, a lean, strong band of muscle flexing below his shirt. 'I'm going for a shower,' he extended, without any expression at all.

Lilah curled up in a ball on one side of the bed, too tired and wrung out to agonise or argue. So that was that? There was to be no further discussion?

Bastien had assumed that she had slept with Josh last night. Did he believe that she hadn't? Did she care whether he believed her or not?

He was so…so…*volatile*. She hadn't been prepared for that—had assumed that deep down inside he was cold as ice and detached. She had been wrong. In addition, only a few hours ago she would have been overcome with embarrassment at the prospect of facing Bastien again. At least she would've been until Bastien himself had dismissed what they had shared as 'innocent', which had certainly clarified matters as far as she was concerned.

Years of standing back and protecting herself while other people dabbled in sex had, she had decided ruefully, made her prudish and naive. As far as Bastien was concerned nothing worthy of note had yet happened between them. Why else would he have called an episode that had shocked her 'innocent'? And if *he* wasn't disturbed or embarrassed by it why should *she* be?

The arrival of a lavish breakfast tray awakened Lilah the next day. She glanced at the dent in the pillow next to her own and marvelled at the reality that she had fallen asleep with Bastien beside her and, in spite of his presence, slept like a log.

She was tucking into a chocolate croissant and covered in crumbs when Berdina, one of Bastien's personal assistants, arrived to tell her that Bastien was in a meeting and that after a brief appointment with

Bastien's lawyer she would be flying to Paris with Bastien in a couple of hours.

While wondering why she was to meet with a lawyer, Lilah packed her new wardrobe and picked out a stylish electric blue coat and fine dress to wear. These designer clothes were props, to support the role that she was being well paid to play, Lilah told herself firmly. Bastien was reopening Moore Components and re-employing the workforce—including her father. That was her payoff. That was why she was with Bastien in the first place.

She needed to remind herself of that reality on a regular basis. There was nothing complicated about their agreement. Bastien had made it all completely straightforward, hadn't he? He wanted her and he had worked out exactly what it would take to persuade her to surrender to his demands. He had proved that she had a price, and she doubted she would ever be able to forgive him for being right about that.

When she emerged from the bedroom the lawyer was waiting to present her with the confidentiality contract that she had agreed to sign.

The older man settled the slim document on the table and Lilah sat down to read it. He drew her attention to various clauses and handed her a pen. It was fairly standard stuff, and after adding her signature she passed the document back.

Porters had arrived to pick up her luggage, and she vacated the hotel in Berdina's company.

'We're lunching with François and Marielle Durand in Paris,' Bastien informed Lilah the instant she sat down opposite him on board his sleek, opulent jet. He wore a charcoal-grey suit, superbly tailored to his lean, powerful frame, and his white shirt framed his strong bronzed jaw.

'Who are they?' Lilah asked curiously.

'Marielle is an ex, now married to François. Including you in the arrangement will make it a more relaxed meeting,' Bastien opined with smooth assurance as coffee was served.

His admission that Marielle Durand was a former lover sent Lilah's interest hurtling into the stratosphere.

'This is for you...' Bastien tossed down a credit card on the table between them. 'While I'm taking care of business this morning you will go shopping, and I'll pick you up when it's time for lunch—'

Lilah studied the credit card with a sinking heart and pushed it away several inches. 'I don't want to spend your money,' she told him tightly.

'I didn't give you a choice. Spending my money goes with the territory and I expect you to do it,' Bastien decreed, flicking the card back towards her with the tip of a forceful finger.

Lilah reminded herself that she didn't have to buy anything and put the card in her clutch bag for the sake of peace. It had not escaped her notice that Bastien's staff watched her every move, visibly curious about her connection with their employer. That interest implied that, from the outside at least, her relationship with Bastien appeared unusual in some way.

She lifted her chin and collided unexpectedly with Bastien's smouldering dark golden eyes. Her temperature rose and her heartbeat thundered, the tip of her tongue sliding out to moisten the dryness of her full lower lip. She was helplessly recalling the expert

stroke of Bastien's fingers over the most intimate part
of her body and reddening to the roots of her hair.

'*Se thelo*… I want you…' Bastien breathed thickly.

Lilah couldn't have found her voice to save herself. Hot colour inflamed her pale complexion, her
eyes widening she gazed back at him, taken aback
by his candour.

A long, tanned forefinger skimmed down the back
of her hand where it rested on the tabletop. 'I've never
waited as long for any woman as I've waited for you.
Of course I'm hot for you. Last night only whetted my
appetite, *koukla mou*.'

As he touched her Lilah tore her gaze from his and
yanked her hand back out of reach. 'You weren't *waiting*,' she told him with tart emphasis, before she could
think better of it. 'Over the past two years you've been
with one woman after another.'

A winged ebony brow climbed. 'Keeping count,
were you?' Bastien quipped.

'Why would *I* care what you do?' Lilah traded,
hot cheeked.

'I don't want you to *care* about me in any way,'
Bastien countered without hesitation, his stunning
dark eyes welded to her expressive face. 'This is sex,
nothing more.'

Lilah lifted a delicate brow. 'What else could it be?'

Walking through the airport in Paris with Bastien,
she was disconcerted to move beyond the barrier and
suddenly find a phalanx of cameras aimed at them.
Dismay gripped her, because the last thing she wanted
was to be publically outed as Bastien Zikos's latest
'hottie'.

In an effort to lessen that risk she stepped away from Bastien and endeavoured to act more like an employee than a lover. The cameras continued to flash regardless. Questions were shouted, asking who she was in both French and English. They, like the photographers, were ignored.

Her colour fluctuating, Lilah climbed into the limo outside the airport accompanied by Berdina, who was to act as her guide on the shopping trip, and Ciro, who was with her for security. By that time Lilah was worrying that her family or her friends would see photos of her with Bastien in the papers and become suspicious that she was doing more than simply working for him.

But once the affair was over would that really matter? she asked herself ruefully.

The car whisked them to the Avenue Montaigne, where a whole range of designer shops were located.

While Berdina's attention was elsewhere Lilah looked up Marielle Durand on her phone. Photos of a slender exquisite blonde cascaded across the screen and Lilah swallowed hard. Marielle had been a famous model before her marriage.

Her thoughts abstracted, Lilah prowled through Louis Vuitton, Dior and Chanel and browsed, before obeying the letter of the law in Ralph Lauren and flourishing Bastien's credit card to buy Bastien a new tie. He couldn't complain now, could he? She had bought something.

Bastien joined her at noon. 'Where are your shopping bags?' he demanded.

Lilah extracted the small package from her clutch and handed it to him. 'For you.'

Bastien frowned at her. 'For...*me*?'

'You said I had to spend your money, so I did.'

Bastien unwrapped the gold silk tie and studied it in astonishment. 'You bought me a tie?'

'I won't need anything new to wear this century, after the amount of stuff you bought in London,' Lilah pointed out.

'That wasn't the point of the exercise,' Bastien traded harshly. 'The point is that, for once, I wanted you to do *exactly* as you were told.'

'Sorry, sir, I'll have to try harder,' Lilah quipped.

'Have you always found it this hard to follow instructions?'

'When *you're* issuing them...yes,' she admitted ruefully.

'You should *want* to please me,' Bastien told her as blue eyes bright as sapphires met his critical gaze.

With her dark hair framing her triangular face and her eyes sparkling above her neat little nose and her full rosy mouth, she looked amazingly fragile and feminine—as well as fizzingly alive.

'Why?'

'It puts me in a better mood.'

While Lilah tried to imagine Bastien's moods influencing her in any way, the limo nosed back into the traffic.

The Durands lived in an imposing eighteenth-century townhouse on Ile Saint-Louis. A maid ushered them into an airy salon, where introductions were performed and drinks were served.

Keenly aware of Marielle Durand's scrutiny, Lilah struggled to relax. Marielle was even more beautiful in the flesh than she had looked in her photographs, and Lilah was surprised to realise that the other woman was English.

Bastien surprised Lilah by closing his hand over hers to keep her close while he chatted to François. The conversation was solely in French, until Marielle addressed Lilah in English and asked her about her home town. Relieved not to be forced to stumble out any more stock phrases in her schoolgirl French, Lilah relaxed a little over the light lunch that was being served.

Over a glass of wine, the beautiful blonde invited Lilah to walk round the garden with her.

'How long have you been with Bastien?' Marielle asked with unconcealed curiosity, as soon as the men were out of earshot.

'Only a few days,' Lilah admitted wryly. 'Am I allowed to ask when you…?'

'Years and years ago—soon after I first made my name in the modelling world. He was probably my most exciting affair,' the other woman confided with an abstracted laugh. 'I adore my husband, but I've never felt anything like the excitement I once felt around Bastien. He's a heartbreaker, though, too damaged to ever trust his heart to one woman and settle down.'

'Damaged?' Lilah queried with a frown.

'Oh, I don't know any details, but I've always been certain he must come from a challenging background. No man's that hard to hold, and no man finds it that impossible to trust a woman without good reason,' Marielle opined. 'He was too complicated for me.'

And then Lilah made a discovery that disconcerted her: she *liked* complicated—actually *enjoyed*

the challenge of wondering what made Bastien tick.
He was like no other man she had ever met. Incalculably clever, impatient, volatile and unpredictable.
He was an unashamed workaholic, evidently unfulfilled by the huge achievements he had already made.
What had made him like that… *Who* had made him
like that? What drove him? And why did she care?

'You charmed the Durands very effectively,' Bastien
pronounced on their journey back to the airport. 'You
don't have a jealous bone in your body where I'm concerned, do you?'

'Why would I?' Lilah parried, quickly overcoming her surprise at that unexpected stab. 'I can't think
you'd welcome a possessive woman.'

That was certainly true, Bastien acknowledged
grudgingly, and yet when he had glanced out through
the patio doors standing open to the sunlight to see
Delilah smiling and laughing, seemingly on the very
best of terms with Marielle, he had been surprisingly
riled by Delilah's complete indifference to his past
history with the beautiful blonde.

The faintest colour warmed Lilah's cheeks, because
although she had not been jealous or possessive she
had felt uncomfortable in Marielle's company—and
positively nauseous at the knowledge that Bastien had
been sexually intimate with her hostess.

'Where are we going now?' she asked, purely to
change the subject.

'I have a chateau in Provence…'

CHAPTER SIX

THEY LEFT THE airport in a rough terrain vehicle, with Bastien at the wheel and his security team following in another car.

The glorious Provençal light was beginning to fade, softening hard edges with shadow. They drove through rugged hills with deep gorges and fertile valleys. The hilltops were scattered with picturesque fortified villages with narrow meandering streets and sleepy shuttered houses. As the landscape grew increasingly spectacular the land became lusher. Ancient vineyards cloaked the sloping hills with ranks of bright green vines, while orchards of peaches, pears, nectarines and cherries flourished on stone terraces.

'Did you inherit the chateau from your family?' Lilah finally asked, unable to stifle her curiosity because Bastien had not offered a shred of further information.

'I'm not from a rich family,' Bastien told her drily. 'My mother was a waitress born in an Athens back street. My father is a small-time property developer who is, admittedly, married to a very wealthy woman. Regrettably, he was never married to *my* mother.'

'Oh…' Lilah responded after an awkward pause.

'When you mentioned your father giving your mother the sea horse pendant, and you thinking that you and your parents were the perfect family, you gave me a very different impression of your background.'

'What I meant was that back then I was still young enough to be ignorant of exactly what their relationship entailed.'

'And what *did* it entail?'

'My father, Anatole, is married to another woman. My mother was his mistress. She once admitted to me that she deliberately chose to become pregnant with me because she believed my father would divorce his wife for her if she gave him a child,' Bastien volunteered in the driest of tones. 'Unhappily for her, her scheme failed—because my father's wife had already conceived my half-brother, Leo, who is only a few months older than I am. My mother was extremely bitter about *that* development.'

'And she *told* you that?' Lilah pressed in consternation.

His beautifully shaped mouth quirked. 'Athene wasn't the maternal type, and she never did overcome her resentment at having the responsibility and expense of a child she no longer had any use for.'

Lilah compressed her full lips, the skin around her mouth bloodless from the force of will it took for her to remain silent in the face of what he was telling her. She was shocked, but she didn't want to admit it, sensing that Bastien would ridicule her revulsion at his mother's callous candour. But no child should know he was unwanted, she thought painfully. No child should have to live with the demeaning knowledge that he had only been conceived to be used as a piece of emotional blackmail in his mother's battle to win a wedding ring from his father.

'No comment? I felt sure you would have several moralising remarks to make.'

'Then you were wrong. I know that all children don't grow up in a picturebook-perfect world,' Lilah breathed tautly. 'Otherwise my father would have loved my mother and stayed faithful to her...'

'He *wasn't*?' Bastien shot her a disconcerted look from frowning dark eyes. 'You're very close to your father. I naturally assumed...'

'My parents weren't happily married. There were always other women in my father's life, and constant upsetting scenes in my home. He didn't love my mother. They'd been together since they were teenagers, though, and everyone expected him to marry her—so eventually he did,' she proffered ruefully. 'It was a long time before I understood that succumbing to that social pressure had made him feel trapped in their marriage. He's a different man with my stepmother.'

'Did your father's infidelity contribute to your judgemental view of me as a "shameless man whore"?' Bastien shot at her, throwing her completely off balance.

Lilah flushed to the roots of her hair at having her own insult flung back at her two years after the event and when she'd least expected it. 'Of course not... However, you *are* a womaniser, Bastien.'

'But *not* a man whore. I have never been unfaithful to a lover,' Bastien asserted levelly. 'I have never taken indiscriminate sexual partners either. While my values may not be the same as yours, I *do* have standards.'

Mortification had claimed Lilah and it was eating her alive. She closed her hands together tightly on her lap. 'I lost my temper that night. I shouldn't have made such personal and disparaging comments to someone I barely knew,' she conceded, hoping that her admission would close the subject.

'Is that an apology?'

Lilah breathed in so deep that her narrow chest swelled.

'I mean,' Bastien mused, and his deep, dark, Greek-accented drawl was as rich as molasses, 'I did only ask you to dine with me and spend the night. I didn't assault you or abuse you.'

Lilah lost her battle with her temper and flung her hands up in a violent demonstration of exasperation. 'All right…all *right*… I'm sorry with bells on! Are you satisfied now?'

Bastien stole an amused glance at the glittering brightness of her eyes above her pink cheeks. 'What would a virgin know about a man whore's lifestyle anyway?' he derided.

Staring rigidly out through the windscreen as the vehicle turned between tall stone pillars to drive down a lane lined on both sides with very tall stately trees, Lilah rolled her eyes. 'Maybe I read a lot of raunchy books…'

Amused against his will, Bastien bit out a rough-edged laugh. She was in the wrong and she knew it—but she still wouldn't back down the way other women did with him. He enjoyed her stubborn streak and the challenge of making her toe the line.

Lights came on as Bastien parked and killed the engine. 'Welcome to the Chateau Sainte-Monique.'

Wall lamps in the form of iron lanterns illuminated the old building, accentuating the warm honey-coloured stone of the façade and the very Provençal violet-blue shutters at the many windows. Gravel interspersed with formal beds of flowers and trees ornamented the frontage.

Lilah climbed out of the car and accompanied Bastien to the entrance. 'So, when did you buy this place?'

'About three years ago. The owner was an elderly countess, whom I met during the course of a land development deal. The first time I saw the chateau I made her an offer, but it was months before she finally agreed to sell. The renovation took another year. I come here when I want to relax and when I can work from home. I stayed here all last month,' Bastien admitted smoothly.

A middle-aged man in a crisply ironed white shirt and bow tie opened the door and greeted them with a smile.

'Stefan and his wife, Marie, take care of everything here,' Bastien informed Lilah after making an introduction, and a lean hand resting at the base of her spine guided her indoors.

The interior was breathtaking. The hall had a chequerboard black-and-white marble floor and surprisingly modern furniture. A huge stone staircase curved up from the ground floor.

Their luggage was being brought in behind them, and Bastien was heading for the stairs, when Stefan opened a door and a familiar little bark of eagerness froze Lilah in place. Stefan grinned as a brown, silky little bundle of flying flapping ears and wriggling body flew at Lilah with a noisy burst of excited barking.

'Yes…yes, I missed you too,' Lilah admitted, crouching down to scoop up the miniature dachshund. She separated him from one of the beloved squeaky toys he liked to carry around in his mouth and attempted to calm him before she put him down again.

As the dog snatched up the toy again and hurtled across to Bastien, Lilah warned him. 'Just ignore Skippy. He'll get the message and leave you in peace…that's what Vickie always did with him. She prefers cats.'

Skippy nudged the toe of Bastien's shoe with his nose, his beady little eyes pleading. Bastien sidestepped the animal to stride on up the stairs, and Lilah watched in dismay as Skippy hurtled in his wake. Stefan moved forward to intercept the little dog, seemingly aware that his employer was not animal-friendly.

Lilah followed Bastien upstairs into a spectacular atmospheric bedroom furnished with a mixture of antique and contemporary pieces. Oyster-coloured silk festooned the windows and tumbled down in opulent swathes from the wrought-iron crown holder above the big bed.

'This is an amazing place,' Lilah whispered, impressed beyond words by the splendour of her surroundings.

'The maids will unpack for you. I'll see you downstairs for dinner in an hour,' Bastien imparted as a man brought in her luggage and two young women in uniform arrived to move the cases into the dressing room visible through an open door.

Lilah hovered uncertainly.

'Dress up...' Bastien lowered his handsome dark head to murmur huskily in her ear. 'Dress up for dinner so that I can enjoy *undressing* you later, *glikia mou.*'

Banners of self-conscious colour brightened Lilah's porcelain-pale complexion as she turned her head to stare up at him. She collided with brilliant dark eyes that glittered like stars in the low light—stunning eyes, ringed by spiky lashes of velvet black. She was mesmerised. He curved long flexible fingers to the side of her face and brought his mouth crashing down on hers.

That kiss was a taste of heaven and a taste of hell in one package. It was heaven because she couldn't get enough of that hot, hungry mouth on hers and hell because she hated the response she couldn't suppress. He released her, staring down at her for a split second in silence, and then swung on his heel and walked out.

Lilah drifted into the marble bathroom, her fingers creeping up to brush her tingling swollen lips, shame and guilt rising like a dark, choking cloud inside her. It would be cruel if he made her *like* having sex with him, she thought wildly. Or would it? Surely that could only be foolish pride talking?

Her rational brain scolded her for the melodrama Bastien could somehow infuse into her very thoughts. Common sense told her that simply accepting that their intimacy was inevitable would make the experience much more manageable for her. After all, she wasn't a masochist, was she?

Sex was supposed to be enjoyable, she reminded herself. But from listening to friends talk about their experiences she knew it often wasn't that great. Once she had done the deed with Bastien she would probably wonder what all the fuss was about, she reflected wryly, because, after all, sex had to be the most ordinary pursuit in the world.

Stripping, she went for a shower, retrieved her cosmetics to do her face and finally returned to the bedroom wrapped in towels. In the dressing room she flicked through the formal wear now hung for her perusal. *Dress up*, Bastien had urged. Humour sparkling in her eyes, she pulled a ballgown from the rail and fanned it out on the bed. It was over the top and theatrical, rather like the chateau, and when she had modelled it she had noticed Bastien's dark golden eyes blaze like banked-down fires.

Bastien stood in the hall, watching Delilah descend the stairs with the glossy grace and dignity of a queen. The dress was amazing—a glistening sheath in peach that hugged her slender body to just below the waist before it flared out into thousands of layers of net that swept the stone steps. Her black hair tumbled in a mane down her back, strands rippling round her triangular face to highlight her bright blue eyes. The tightening swelling at his groin was so instant he didn't even question his reaction.

He stretched out a lean-fingered brown hand to greet Lilah as she reached the foot of the stairs, his arrogant dark head thrown back, smouldering dark golden eyes locking to the full pink pout of her lush mouth. He closed his fingers round hers.

'In that dress you take my breath away,' he told her.

Her mouth ran dry as she met his gaze and her

small breasts swelled below the skin-tight bodice as she gulped in oxygen. She hadn't expected that blunt compliment, didn't know how to deal with it.

He walked her through an airy salon, with an ancient stone carved fireplace and sleek blue sofas, out on to a tiled terrace where a candlelit table awaited them.

'I'm really hungry,' Lilah confessed as a manservant moved forward to pull out a chair and lingered to whisk a napkin across her lap.

'You should enjoy the meal. Stefan's wife, Marie, is my cook, and she was a chef in a Michelin-starred restaurant in Paris before they came to work for me,' Bastien remarked while the wine was poured.

'You have a huge staff here…you live like a king,' Lilah commented helplessly as soon as they were alone.

'I do when I have the time to enjoy the chateau— which is rarely,' Bastien qualified drily. 'When I'm travelling on business I eat out or cook for myself.'

'You can *cook*?' Lilah said in surprise.

'Of course I can. I'm not spoilt. I've never been spoilt. But I do appreciate the best things in life.'

'Is your mother still alive?' she asked abruptly as the first course was served.

Bastien studied her in silence, black brows drawing together in a frown. 'You're very curious about my life.'

Lilah shrugged her lightly clad shoulder. 'Why wouldn't I be?'

Bastien set down his glass. 'My mother died in a car accident when I was a child and I had to go and live with my father.'

Lilah toyed with the artfully presented courgette flowers topping the tiny onion tart on her plate. 'And how was that?'

'Hideous,' Bastien admitted grimly. 'Anatole's wife, Cleta, hated me on sight. I was the living proof of her husband's infidelity. As for my half-brother... Leo was an adored only child and suddenly I turned up. Naturally he resented me. But there were some advantages to my new home,' he conceded, his dark eyes veiled with mystery, his beautiful mouth compressing.

'Such as...?' The sliver of onion tart Lilah had selected was melting in her mouth.

Bastien frowned at her continuing interest. 'It was a fresh start for me in many ways. I was able to see Anatole regularly and I went to a much better school.'

'Obviously you're close to your father,' Lilah commented, relieved to hear that hint of indulgent warmth in his dark drawl when he referred to his parent, because really it was brutally obvious to her that Bastien had been cursed by the most utterly miserable childhood.

'Yes. I'm very fond of Anatole. He may have been a push-over for the wrong women, but as a father, when I needed him, he was the very best,' Bastien stated with quiet pride.

Relief filled Lilah that there had been someone loving in Bastien's life, and she wondered why the idea of nobody having cared for him as a child should disturb her so much. His answers to her questions, however, had given her a certain insight into what had made him so tough and unyielding.

'But that's enough about my life, *glikia mou*,' Bastien continued, smooth as glass. 'Tell me about Josh Burrowes.'

Thrown off balance in her turn, Lilah stiffened, her spine straightening. 'There's nothing to tell. We were on the same course at uni. He's one of my friends.'

Bastien lounged back in his seat as their plates were cleared and the main course served. 'But obviously Josh wants to be something more. You should've told him the truth.'

Lilah's delicate bone structure tightened. 'I gave my friends the same story you suggested I use with my family. I said you'd offered me a job.'

Bastien rested his shimmering dark gaze on the voluptuous promise of her pink lips as she savoured the tender lamb on her plate. 'But you should have come clean for Josh's benefit and told him that you are *mine*.'

Her small white teeth gritted as if she had trodden barefoot on a stone. 'I am *not* yours, Bastien.'

'You *are*,' Bastien purred in immediate contradiction, his accented drawl vibrating through her slender taut frame. 'I know it every time I look at you. No hunger this powerful is one-sided.'

Lilah concentrated on her meal, deeming silence the most diplomatic response. She was very, *very* attracted to him, she admitted inwardly, but no way did she owe him that amount of truth.

As she studied him a snaking curl of warmth stirred low in her pelvis and something tightened even deeper inside her, making her shift uneasily in her seat. The hard, masculine lines of his compellingly beautiful face and the suppressed ferocity of his stunningly intense eyes welded her attention to him.

The first time she had seen Bastien she had known

that she had never seen a more beautiful male speci-
men, and in the two years that had since passed that
fact remained the absolute truth. Bastien was gorgeous. She knew it and he had to know it too.

Perspiration beaded her short upper lip, and as a
member of staff stepped up to the table to refresh their
wine glasses she finally dragged her attention from
Bastien and breathed in deep.

'Stefan's wife is a fantastic chef,' she remarked,
after savouring the first mouthful of a roasted pear
dessert served with chocolate sauce and then pushing the plate away in defeat. 'But I can't find room
for another bite…'

'Coffee?' Bastien prompted.

'No, thanks…' Lilah tensed as he rose fluidly out of
his seat and strolled, jungle-cat-graceful, towards her.

'I react like a teenager around you,' Bastien murmured thickly. 'I can't wait one minute longer.'

Lilah pushed her hands down on the table-edge and
levered herself upright, the layers of her dress spilling out round her in peach abundance. *Time to pay
the piper*, she thought crazily.

Bastien didn't immediately touch her. Instead he
lowered his dark head and circled her mouth almost
teasingly with his own, touching delicate nerve-
endings that screamed with awareness to send pulses
of heat shooting down through her. Her head swam a
little…her knees wobbled.

With a guttural sound low in his throat, Bastien
swept her up in his arms.

'I was so angry with you last night when I heard
about you kissing Josh,' he told her unexpectedly as
he carried her up the stone staircase, contriving that

feat as easily as if she weighed no more than a child.
'Don't let another man touch you in any way while
you're with me.'

Her senses still drowning from that extraordinarily
intoxicating kiss, Lilah looked up at him with dazed
blue eyes and blinked. 'Not much risk of that.'

'Why not? You're a beauty. I saw it... *Josh* saw it,'
he grated in harsh reminder.

'But you see things in me that I don't,' she muttered uncomfortably, thinking of the conventionally
beautiful fashion models he generally took to his bed.

In comparison, *she* was an aberration. Each and
every one of her predecessors that she had seen had
been tall, blonde and classically lovely, with Marielle the perfect example of that ideal. Lilah, however,
was small and kind of skinny. She had certainly been
way too skinny and small in the bust and hip department for any of the boys to look at while she was at
school, at an age where having curves had seemed so
very important.

'I know that I want you,' Bastien spelt out. 'Everything else fades in the face of that.'

'Everything?' Lilah questioned in disbelief.

'Everything...' Bastien husked, breathing in the
coconut scent of her shampoo, the faint aroma of the
cosmetics she had applied, the fragrance that was
uniquely and alluringly hers. And those eyes, he savoured, those sapphire-blue eyes that shone like jew-
els...

He settled her down on the bed in her room, and
the hunger driving him spooked him more than just
a little as he looked down at her. That hunger would
fade as soon as he'd had her, he told himself cyni-

cally, and in all likelihood even the sex would be a disappointment. How could it be otherwise when she had no experience? She couldn't possibly be a truly sensual woman, his rational mind assured him. No truly sensual woman could have stayed untouched as long as she had. She might light up when he looked at her, move in his arms as though she were a sensually aware woman, but it was unlikely that she would have much to offer.

He plucked off her shoes, resisting a decidedly warped urge to stroke those tiny feet of hers. Her virginity was unsettling him, Bastien decided, desperate to suppress the strange thoughts and reactions assailing him. But if she was telling him the truth—and he had to believe it *was* the truth—she would be more his than any other woman had ever been. And for some peculiar reason he liked that idea, he acknowledged in bewilderment. He *really* liked that idea.

'What are you thinking about?' Lilah whispered awkwardly as he ran down the zip on her dress.

'Sex. What else?'

'So I asked a stupid question…deal with it,' Lilah cut back without skipping a beat.

Above her head, an unholy grin slashed Bastien's firmly modelled mouth. He eased the dress off a slight white shoulder and rolled the sleeves down her slim arms, completely attuned to the rising tempo of her breathing.

'I'm not going to harm you,' Bastien breathed with husky assurance. 'Not in any way.'

'I've heard it can hurt,' Lilah told him stubbornly.

'You make the prospect of having sex with me

sound like some form of medieval torture,' Bastien growled.

'I'm going to shut up now. Zipping my mouth,' Lilah spelt out jerkily.

Bastien tugged off the dress and tossed it in a careless heap on the carpet.

'I saw the price tag on that dress, Bastien. You can't treat it like that…it's indecent!'

Bastien flung back his handsome dark head and laughed out loud. 'I thought you were zipping it? Keep quiet…you're making me nervous.'

'What have *you* got to be nervous about?' Lilah demanded in wonderment.

She was finding it a huge challenge not to simply dive below the sheets. There she was, with her body on display, skinny as a rail, clad only in little pale pink lacy pieces of lingerie, and she was being forced to pose like some pantomime seductress on a silk-clad bed. Goosebumps rose on her exposed skin.

Bastien slid a hand into his pocket and withdrew a jewel box. 'This is for you.'

Lilah sat up and took the opportunity to hug her knees, covering up her all-too-bare body as best she could. 'I don't want gifts, Bastien.'

'You will wear it to please me, *koukla mou*. The first time I saw you I wanted to see you in diamonds.' Bastien flipped open the lid on an exquisite shimmering diamond pendant on a chain. He removed it from the box and clasped it round her slender neck.

Taken aback, Lilah didn't move a muscle as he put the pendant on her, feeling the diamond settle cold and heavy against her chilled skin. Bastien stepped back from the bed to remove his jacket and unbutton his shirt, but the whole time his attention was fixed to her.

Lilah met dark golden eyes, tawny as a lion's, and her skin blazed as though he had set her on fire, all sense of being cool in temperature and cold with nerves instantly evaporating. Beneath his bronzed skin he flexed washboard abs and well-developed pectoral muscles, which made her stare for a second or two. He was what a friend had once described as 'built'—powerfully masculine in every way.

She glanced away as his long, tanned fingers reached for the waistband of his trousers, cursing her shyness, her awful self-consciousness with her own body, never mind his. He tossed some foil packets down by the bed, and the nape of her neck prickled.

He came down on the bed still in his boxers, and with the flick of a finger unfastened her wispy bra and pulled it away. She felt her nipples bead, tightening into pointed peaks, and then all of a sudden, or so it seemed to her in her heightened state of nerves, he was laying her down against the pillows and touching those agonisingly sensitive buds with his mouth and his fingers.

A little shudder racked her, and then another. Sensation was breaking through her defences as her breasts tingled and swelled, responding to his attention.

'At least put out the light!' she exclaimed.

'You're beautiful. I need to look at you.'

'I don't want you looking,' she gritted between clenched teeth.

'Close your eyes and pretend I'm not,' Bastien suggested.

Sniping back at him became an impossibility while he was tracing a trail down her slender body with his mouth—kissing here, licking there, discovering the areas of her midriff that responded to his blatant teasing with wild enthusiasm and then slowly shifting down to more intimate areas. His fingers tugged at the waist of her knickers and she stopped breathing. She felt his breath on her...*there*...where it shouldn't be. He found the most achingly sensitive place of all with his clever fingers, and her hips jerked and her breath hitched and she closed her eyes, blocking out the bedroom while becoming even more insanely aware of Bastien's every move.

'You're really practised at this, aren't you?' Lilah commented gruffly.

'We're not about to pursue that subject.'

'No... *Oh!*' A strangled exclamation broke involuntarily from her lips as he stroked his tongue across the little nub of nerve-endings at the apex of her thighs.

With a strangled groan, Bastien came up over her again and crushed her parted lips under his, his tongue plunging only once, but deep, into the moist interior of her mouth, somehow igniting a ball of heat in her pelvis. Startled blue eyes flew wide and clashed with gold circled by lush black lashes.

'Oh...' Bastien said for her, with a wolfish grin that made her tummy flip in a somersault.

Feeling like a child who had foolishly stuck her hand in the fire, Lilah closed her eyes again circumspectly. He punished her by returning to his former activity, his fingertips grazing the inside of her slender thighs, where she had never been touched, and every single point of contact tingled and fired hot, like a burn. He used his mouth on her clitoris and it felt unbearably good, with sensation firing through her on all cylinders as the little tickles and prickles of uncontrollable pleasure mounted and she could no longer stay still. Her neck extended and her hips shifted and rose.

Bastien was touching her so gently. She had not imagined that he could be gentle in bed—had, in truth, been braced for passion, aggression and impatience. He slid a finger into her tight sheath and then another…tender, subtle, tormentingly pleasurable. Her blood was pounding in her veins, her heart was racing, and her whole body was damp with perspiration because everything she was feeling had swiftly become so shockingly intense.

She gave up on the losing battle to resist and opened her mouth on a gasp of reaction. Indeed, she was all reaction now, as waves of response coursed through her in an unstoppable tide. Every tiny caress and exploration he executed engulfed her in another wash of sensation. A tight feeling nestled at the heart of her and she shifted impatiently up towards Bastien, fighting the hollow sense of tortured frustration he had awakened without even fully grasping what it was.

'Bastien!' she exclaimed.

Burnished golden eyes assailed hers. 'Tell me you want me.'

'You know I do!' she flared, with a bitterness she couldn't hide.

'You always did, didn't you?' Bastien grated.

'What do you want? A trophy?' Lilah gasped.

'You *are* my trophy,' Bastien told her, his skilled fingertips moving with expert precision at her tender core and setting off a chain reaction inside her.

The mushroom of heat penned inside Lilah suddenly surged up, with a force that blindsided her and overflowed. Out of her control, her body bucked and twisted and convulsed as the paroxysms of a powerful climax rippled through her slender frame.

Bastien ripped open a foil packet with his strong white teeth. He didn't want to hurt her, he didn't want to harm her in any way, but now she was as wet and receptive as she would ever be. He dragged a pillow under her to tip her hips up more and settled between her spread thighs.

The pleasure Bastien had meted out was like a powerful drug that took time to wear off. Lilah was still in a daze when she felt the pressure of Bastien's entry stretching her tender flesh. Apprehension made her stiffen, a heartbeat before the sharp sting of his full possession made her catch her breath on a huff of dismay. He withdrew, hooked her legs higher and thrust into her yielding body again. This time there was no pain—only the amazing sensation of his fullness inside her.

'It's not hurting,' she told him in relief.

A sheen of perspiration dampened Bastien's lean, handsome features—for such care, such temperate precision, had not come without cost. 'Se thelo…you feel unbelievable, hara mou.'

He rolled his hips in a wicked snaking motion that sent extraordinary sensation flooding through Lilah's pelvis, and her eyes went wide with surprise. As he began to move, the first jolt of excitement careened through her without warning, and then the heat and pressure at the heart of her began to build again. It was a little like hitching a ride on a comet, she thought dizzily, with new responses released and overwhelming her.

Hunger sank talon claws of need into her very bones. Her heart slammed against her ribcage. Her body thrummed and pulsed with rippling darts of pleasure that only stoked her rising hunger. And then the intensity climbed to an unbearable height and pushed her over into the intoxicating grip of wave after wave of sweet, drowning pleasure.

It was over…it was done, Lilah reflected in a daze, crazily conscious of the crash of Bastien's heart against hers, the brush of his hair against her cheek, the dampness of his big, powerful body against hers, the sheer weight of him and the incredible intimacy of their position. Well, she had no complaints, she conceded thoughtfully. In fact, he had made the experience amazing.

In the process of rebooting, after the longest, hottest climax in his considerable experience, Bastien breathed again. He rolled off her and caught her back into his arms, pressing a kiss to her brow without even thinking about it…

And then the thinking kicked in hard. What the hell was he doing? What the hell was he playing at? He didn't *do* touchy-feely—never had and never would. True, she had just given him a pleasure he was finding hard to match in his memory, and he already knew he wanted her again. But it was in the way an alcoholic knew he wanted a drink.

The comparison jarred, but it worked its magic, and Bastien pulled away from the strangely tempting pleasure of having her small, slender body lying against his. He sprang out of bed and headed for the bathroom.

'I'm a restive sleeper and I prefer my own space,' he told her carelessly. 'I'll be sleeping in the room next door.'

Lilah could feel herself freeze with regret and discomfiture. Yet such separation was what sex without caring was like, she scolded herself. It was a bodily thing—not a mental thing. Bastien didn't feel any deep connection with her. He had satisfied his lust for the moment and that was that: he had leapt out of bed and straight into the shower. She could already hear it running.

Had she expected a warmer conclusion to their intimacy?

Well, if she had expected that she was an idiot. After all, wasn't this exactly why she had lost her temper with Bastien two years back? He had only offered sex when she had wanted more, and that had hurt—hurt her pride, hurt her heart too. Wasn't it time she was honest about that? She had started falling for Bastien Zikos the first moment she'd laid eyes on his fallen angel face and stunning eyes.

Of course she hadn't known him in any way, so it had been infatuation rather than love, but his magnetic attraction had called to her on every level. And resisting it, recognising that he could only make her unhappy, had cut deep and filled her with disappointment. But it was the truth and it remained the truth, Lilah conceded ruefully. Bastien skated along happily on the shallow side of life, taking pleasure where he chose, discarding women whenever he got bored... and now she was one of those passing fancies—a sexual whim.

She shifted in the bed, and the ache between her

thighs made her wince and grimace. Once she had said no to Bastien, and evidently that had put a price beyond rubies on her head because he wasn't used to the word *no* and evidently couldn't live with it.

Stop thinking these negative thoughts—stop it, she screamed inside her head, shifting on the pillow as if to clear it. It would be better to concentrate on the positive—think of the factory up and running again, her father back in his office and her little half-siblings secure because their parents were no longer worried sick about how to pay their bills. That was a *good* picture, she told herself soothingly.

And what about all Moore's former employees? Her father had mentioned that he'd be calling a meeting on site today, to discuss the relocation of the factory and the planned reopening. That news would make a lot of people very happy.

Indeed, only a very sad, total loser would sit feeling sorry for herself when she was surrounded by so many positive reminders of what sacrificing her pride had achieved. And she *wasn't* a loser, she told herself angrily, and she *wasn't* going to make a big dramatic deal out of what couldn't be changed. So she had had sex with Bastien—that was all it had been and she could live with that reality.

Sliding out of bed, she walked naked into the dressing room and extracted a robe, knotting the sash at her waist with impatient hands.

As she walked back towards the bathroom, Bastien emerged from it, lean bronzed hips swathed in a towel. Crystalline drops of water sprinkled his hair-roughened chest and his thick black hair curled back damply from his brow.

Seeing her out of bed, he frowned. 'I thought you'd be sleeping.'

'No. I need to shower.' To wash his touch and the memory of it away, Lilah thought frantically, colliding with smouldering golden eyes framed by velvet dark lashes and feeling her heart skipping an entire beat. A shadow of faint black stubble accentuated his hard masculine jawline and his beautifully modelled sensual mouth.

As Delilah attempted to sidestep him, Bastien shot out a hand to enclose her wrist and force her to a halt again. 'You were amazing, *glikia mou*,' he husked.

Mortification drummed up hot below Lilah's skin, but she lifted her tousled head high. 'It wasn't as bad as I thought it would be,' she admitted prosaically, tugging her wrist free to continue on past into the bathroom.

Taken aback, Bastien blinked. How to damn with faint praise, he reflected grimly, thrusting open the communicating door between the bedrooms to stride into his own. And how very typical of Delilah to sting him like a wasp.

Well, what else had Bastien expected from her? Lilah asked herself as she washed. Compliments?

She had told him the truth, even though she knew that she hadn't been strictly fair. He could have been more selfish and less careful with her in bed. To give credit where it was due, he *had* made an effort not to hurt her. Unfortunately his consideration in that respect could not eradicate the ugly fact that Bastien Zikos had blackmailed her into his bed. Yes, she had made the choice to accept his unscrupulous deal, but he could not expect her to start treating him like a much-appreciated and personally chosen lover, could he?

Lilah fell into an exhausted sleep, but Bastien was awakened by a phone call at an ungodly early hour of the following morning and given the kind of news that wrecked both his day and his mood.

CHAPTER SEVEN

'DELILAH!' BASTIEN GRATED from the doorway. 'Get up—I need to talk to you...'

Wondering what she had done to deserve such a rude awakening, Lilah opened her eyes only wide enough to peer at the pretty miniature alarm clock adorning the bedside cabinet. It was barely seven in the morning.

Blinking rapidly, in an effort to get her brain functioning again, she swallowed back a yawn and struggled to focus on Bastien's tall, powerful figure by the door that appeared to communicate between her room and his. 'What's wrong?' she asked sleepily.

'We'll discuss it when you get up,' Bastien framed darkly, glittering dark eyes settling on her with chilling distaste. 'I'll see you downstairs in five minutes.'

Exasperated, Lilah rolled her eyes. In mega-bossy mode, Bastien infuriated her—and she refused to be ordered round like an unruly schoolgirl. On the other hand, something bad had clearly happened, and he evidently thought she was involved in it in some way—because why else would he have looked at her as if she had just crawled out from under a stone? Even so…he expected her downstairs within *five minutes*? In his dreams!

Scrambling out of bed, she went into the dressing room and searched through innumerable drawers to find her own humble clothing, from which she selected denim shorts and a simple white tank top to deal with the early-morning heat she could feel in the air. Following a quick shower and the application of a little light make-up, Lilah stalked downstairs in flat canvas shoes, ready for whatever Bastien might choose to throw at her.

With a noisy scrabbling of his claws on the hallway tiles, Skippy hurled himself at Lilah's knees. Stefan informed her that Bastien was waiting for her in his study and directed her down a corridor. Breakfast, he added helpfully, would be served out on the terrace.

Bastien was lodged by the window of a large, imposing book-lined room with his broad back turned towards her. Muscles flexed beneath the taut, expensive fabric of his jacket. He swung round, and she was irritated that she immediately noted that his dark designer suit acted as a superb tailored frame for his wide shoulders, narrow hips and long, powerful thighs.

Hard, dark golden eyes zeroed in on her, and involuntarily, Lilah paled at the intensity of that tough, questioning scrutiny.

Mouth curling, Bastien scanned her appearance in the worn shorts and casual top, neither of which had featured in her officially sanctioned new wardrobe. The adolescent outfit combined with her long, tumbled hair and only a touch of make-up made her look very much like a teenager. Admittedly, though, an incredibly pretty teenager.

Pretty...an old-fashioned word which didn't belong in his vocabulary, Bastien reflected in exasperation at his lack of concentration. *Hot* would be a more appropriate word, and from the top of her curly dark head down to her pert breasts, tiny waist and slim sexy legs and the very soles of her tiny canvas-shod feet, Delilah looked amazingly hot.

He tensed, reluctant to embrace that thought, but his body was already doing that for him, reacting with libidinous enthusiasm to her presence.

'What's this all about?' she asked in apparent innocence.

In answer, Bastien crossed the room and lifted his tablet from the desk top. *'This!'* he bit out wrathfully.

Lilah moved closer to stare at the British newspaper headline depicted on the screen.

Dufort Pharmaceuticals to join Zikos stable?

'I still don't know what you're talking about,' Lilah pointed out, although she had the vaguest recollection that she *had* heard that company's name mentioned during Bastien's deliberations with his staff that first evening in the hotel in London. Unfortunately, since she had not really been listening, she had not the foggiest idea why Bastien was so annoyed.

'Someone leaked confidential information to the press that night in London...and I believe it was *you*!' Bastien breathed with raw emphasis.

Lilah's spine snapped straight as an arrow, her blue eyes rounding with disbelief as she tipped her head back to look him in the eye. *'Me?'* she spluttered incredulously. 'Are you nuts?'

His cool, sculpted mouth hardened. 'You're the only person who left the suite during my discussions with the team that evening. According to my sources, someone tipped off the press halfway through that evening. The bodyguard accompanying you saw you making several phone calls. You also had contact with a journalist.'

Her soft mouth had fallen open in shock, because she could barely credit what she was hearing. How dared he accuse her of being some sort of business spy when he had shared a bed with her the night before? How *dared* he?

Her colour rose even higher when she recalled that he had actually slept apart from her, and she replied curtly, 'I can't believe you're serious. Why would you suspect me of stealing confidential information? Why would anyone want to leak it?'

'The tip that I'm planning to buy Dufort Pharmaceuticals is worth hundreds of thousands of pounds on the open market.'

'But I didn't leak it. I didn't discuss it with anyone,' Lilah remonstrated. 'Why would I have? Apart from anything else, I'm not interested in that information and I wasn't really listening to what you and your staff were talking about… I was watching TV.'

'You were present throughout. You heard *everything*,' Bastien reminded her obdurately.

'At least four members of your staff were present as well! Why are you picking on *me*?' Lilah demanded in a furious counter-attack.

'I have absolute faith in my personal team.'

'I'm delighted to hear it, but obviously your faith is misplaced in at least *one* of them,' Lilah pointed out thinly. 'Because I can assure you that *I* didn't sell any information about your business dealings to anyone.'

'I don't trust you,' Bastien admitted harshly, because he had looked at the evidence from every angle and the conclusion that Delilah had sold the information made the most sense.

Lilah set the tablet back down on the table. 'Well, I'm not playing the fall guy, here, so you have a problem. I suggest you stop wasting time suspecting me of doing the dirty on you and search out the real mole. Why would you suspect me anyway? I've got too much to lose in this situation.'

'How?' Bastien gritted, unimpressed, and particularly outraged because he had wakened to the phone call forewarning him of the press release with a powerful craving to enjoy her small slender body again.

'You gave my father a job, which means a lot to him. I wouldn't do anything to jeopardise his continuing employment,' Lilah argued vehemently. 'I'm not an idiot, Bastien. If I betrayed your trust you wouldn't stick to our agreement.'

His hard mouth set into a grim, clenched line, Bastien said nothing. He could not count on her loyalty. She was a woman, not an employee, and she might well want to punish him for the choice he had offered her. That gave her a good motive, and she had certainly had the opportunity that night to pass on news of his acquisition plans for Dufort Pharmaceuticals.

Worst of all, the damage was done now that the facts were out in the public domain. Either he paid through the nose to acquire a company which was no longer the bargain it had been or he decided to back off altogether.

'You have cost me a great deal of money,' Bastien told her harshly.

'You don't *listen*. You haven't listened to a single word I've said in my own defence, have you?' Lilah accused, her eyes flaring an almost other-worldly blue with suppressed rage. 'But I'll say it one more time... *not guilty*. I didn't gossip about your business plans or pass them on to anyone who could profit from knowing about them. I made two separate phone calls after leaving the hotel suite—one to my father and the other to my stepmother. On neither call did I mention your business discussions. The journalist who approached me was a gossip columnist, *not* a financial reporter...' Her voice trailed off as she studied his lean, darkly handsome face, which was shuttered and forbidding. 'You're *still* not listening to me...'

Seething resentment was flaming up through the temper which Lilah was struggling to keep under control. Her hands closed into punitive fists. Even before she had answered his charges she had clearly been judged and found guilty, which was hideously unfair.

'Tell me, do you distrust *all* women or just me?' she slammed.

'Women are very clever at establishing a man's weaknesses and playing on them,' Bastien countered.

'And your only weakness is protecting your profit margins?' Lilah folded her arms defensively and breathed in slow and deep. 'What you really need, Bastien, is a proper challenge.'

The lush black lashes enhancing his gorgeous eyes

lifted, to reveal glittering dark gold chips full of stark enquiry. 'Meaning…?'

'All bets are off between us until you find out who *did* betray your trust and you clear my name.'

'*Diavelos*…what are you trying to say?' Bastien demanded curtly.

'No sex until you sort this out,' Lilah told him in the baldest possible terms. 'I refuse to sleep with a man who thinks I'm some sort of thief and fraudster.'

Dark colour accentuated the exotic line of Bastien's supermodel cheekbones. 'That is *not* what our agreement entails and nor is it an accurate version of what I said to you.'

'Stuff the agreement!' Lilah flung back at him wildly. 'You can't make the kind of accusation you just made and then act like it shouldn't make a difference to me. You check out every employee who was there that night, and anyone else who knew about your interest in that company, you find out who sold you down the river…and then you *apologise* to me.'

Bastien sent her an incredulous glance, dark eyes flashing the purest gold, pride and anger etching taut hard lines into his lean, darkly handsome features. 'Apologise?'

'Yes, you *will* apologise—even if it *kills* you!' Lilah launched at him full volume, all control of her temper abandoned in the face of such wanton provocation. 'You have deeply insulted me, and I refuse to accept that kind of treatment. And, by the way, you can keep this…' Digging the diamond pendant out of her pocket, Lilah set it down on the table. 'I didn't ask for it, I don't appreciate it, and I will not wear it again unless you apologise to me!'

'Are you finished?' Bastien demanded wrathfully. 'I don't *do* apologies.'

'Fortunately it's never too late to learn good manners!' Lilah stated without hesitation, before turning on her heel with Skippy following close behind like a shadow.

She walked out to the shaded terrace for the breakfast Stefan had promised her.

She was trembling when she collapsed down limply into a seat by the table, but she didn't regret a word she had said to Bastien. She had to be tough to deal with him or he would roar over her like a fireball and burn her to ashes in his wake. Bastien had questioned her integrity, and Lilah was proud of her integrity. She was no angel, but she didn't lie, cheat or defraud, or go behind people's backs to score or make a profit, she thought angrily.

It shook her that he could misjudge her to such an extent even after they had become lovers. And that she should even *have* that thought warned her that she was still being very naïve about the nature of their relationship. Their bodies had connected—*not* their minds. Bastien did not know her in the way she had always assumed her first lover would know her. But did that excuse him for assuming on the flimsiest of evidence that she would sneakily sell confidential information about his business plans?

She was already convinced that Bastien did not hold a very high opinion of women—at least not those who shared his bed. She shuddered as she remembered the cold, heavy feel of that brilliant glittering diamond at her throat the night before. Did he believe that expensive gifts of diamonds would excuse bad behaviour? Had other women taught him that?

Nibbling little bites of a chocolate croissant and sipping fresh tea, Lilah tried to be realistic about Bastien. He was incredibly good-looking and incredibly rich…and incredibly good in bed, she affixed, hot-cheeked. For many women his wealth alone would be sufficient to excuse almost all character flaws. Not that it would bother Bastien that *she* was unwilling to overlook those flaws, Lilah reflected ruefully, because Bastien was only interested in sex.

And every time she came back to that salient fact it was like crashing into a solid brick wall, which concluded all further speculation.

Having eaten, she asked Stefan for a bottle of water and went off to explore, with Skippy bouncing in excitement round her feet. She could not contemplate sitting around in the chateau submissively, as if she was waiting for Bastien to vindicate her or justify her very existence.

The gardens surrounding the chateau were typically French and formal, lined with precise low box hedges and sculpted topiary set off with immaculate paths, weathered urns and gravel. She balanced like a dancer to walk the edge of an old stone fountain, sending shimmering water drops down into the basin below.

From above, Bastien watched her from a window in the huge first-floor salon. Delilah was larking about like a leggy child, while repeatedly throwing that damned stupid squeaky toy for her even sillier yappy little dog. Delilah outraged his sense of order—

because he did not like the unexpected, and in every way she kept on tossing him the unexpected.

He was willing to admit that she was not behaving like a guilty woman. At the same time he knew women who could act the most legendary Hollywood stars off the screen. His own mother had always put on an impressively deceptive show for his father, who had adored Athene to the bitter end.

But while Anatole had been easily fooled Bastien had always had a low opinion of human beings in general, and he preferred hard truths to polite lies and social pretences. He had also learned that the richer he became, the more people tried to take advantage of him, and he was always on the watch for false flattery and sexual or financial inducements.

In fact, when anyone injured Bastien he hit back twice as hard to punish them and teach them respect. He was not weak. He was not foolish. He was not forgiving. That had been his mantra growing up, when he had had to prove to his own satisfaction that he was stronger than the feeble but kindly father he loved. No woman would ever make a fool out of Bastien Zikos as his mother had made a fool out of his father.

His mother, Athene, had ridiculed his father, calling him 'Mr Sorry', because every time Anatole had visited his mistress and his son he had invariably been grovelling and apologising for something, in a futile effort to keep the peace in the double life of infidelity he led. That was why Bastien was unaccustomed to making apologies of any kind. To his way of thinking, apologies stank to high heaven—of weakness, deceit and cowardly placation.

But at that precise moment Bastien was shocked

to acknowledge that he had not thought through the likely consequences of choosing to confront Delilah immediately about the newspaper leak. Shouldn't he have kept his suspicions to himself until he had established definitive proof? Why the hell had he lost his temper with her like that? Loss of temper meant loss of focus and control, and invariably delivered a poor result. That was why he never allowed himself to lose his temper. Yet on two separate occasions now he had gone off like a rocket with Delilah. Naturally she was playing the innocent and offended card—what else could she do?

'I'll check out every member of your team,' declared Manos, his chief of security, in receipt of his employer's instructions. 'I'm aware that Miss Moore had the opportunity, but somehow she doesn't seem the type.'

'*Is* there a type?' Bastien asked drily, his attention locked to the sway of Delilah's shapely derrière in those tight, faded shorts and the slender perfection of her thighs below the ragged hems.

His fingertips tingled at the idea of trailing those shorts off her slender body and settling her under him again. He cut off that incendiary image and hoped she wasn't planning to leave the grounds dressed in so provocative an outfit.

His strong white teeth gritted. His continuing sexual hunger for Delilah had made her important to Bastien in a way he utterly despised. If she realised how much he was still lusting after her she would use it against him—of course she would. He much preferred the immediate boredom that usually settled in for him after a fresh sexual conquest. He needed to move on, he told himself urgently. He needed to move on from Delilah Moore in particular...*fast*.

The morning flew past while he worked, furiously trying to counteract the damage done by this morning's news report. He went downstairs for lunch and discovered that he had the terrace all to himself, Delilah having opted to have a simple snack in her room. His teeth gritted again and he studied Skippy, lying in a panting heap in the shadows. She had evidently roved far enough around the estate to totally exhaust the dog, which admittedly had pitifully short, stumpy legs.

After a moment's contemplation of the miniature dachshund's lolling pink tongue, Bastien emptied some fruit out of a bowl and poured water into it before putting it down for the animal. Skippy lurched up and drank in noisy gulps. After trotting back indoors, he reappeared with his squeaky toy in his mouth and laid it tenderly at Bastien's feet...where it was ignored.

Full of restive energy, Lilah paced her room. Was she supposed to be a prisoner at the chateau? She refused to sit around and wait as if she had no existence without Bastien to direct her every move.

Recalling the pretty little village of Lourmarin, which they had passed through shortly before their arrival, she decided that what she really needed was an afternoon of sightseeing. Having washed the dust off her canvas-shod feet, she pulled on a white sun dress and sandals before heading downstairs to find Stefan and ask if it was possible for her to visit the village.

Within minutes a car drew up outside to collect

her, and she skipped down the steps, smiling at Ciro as he slid in beside the driver.

Bastien was disconcerted when he discovered that Delilah had left the chateau. He hadn't expected that. Frustration at the childish avoidance tactics she was using on him coursed through him, and he had Manos check with her driver. He set out for Lourmarin in a short temper.

What *was* it about Delilah? She was a lot of trouble, demanding so much more effort and attention from him than other women did. *Why* was he allowing her to wind him up? And why did he still want her, regardless of how much she annoyed him?

It was market day in Lourmarin, and Bastien's disposition was not improved by a lengthy search for a parking spot.

When he tracked Delilah down he heard her laughter first, and even that contrived to annoy him—because two years had passed since *he* had last heard her laugh. In addition, although he hated gigglers, there had always been something incredibly infectious about Delilah's giggles. He saw her seated on a café terrace, her white dress spilling round her, black hair framing her animated face as she laughed and chattered to Ciro, at one point even touching the younger man's arm with a familiarity that set Bastien's teeth on edge.

Ciro, not surprisingly, wore a slack-jawed expression of masculine admiration.

'Delilah...'

The sound of that deep, dark drawl banished the pleasure of Lilah's sun-drenched surroundings and stiffened her spine as much as if a poker had been attached to it. She lifted her head and fell into the smouldering golden sensuality of Bastien's intent scrutiny. His dark-fallen-angel face was grim, but nothing could detract from the sheer beauty of it, nor the mesmeric potency of his gaze.

'Been looking for me?' she quipped, setting down her glass of wine. 'I doubt that your presence here is an unlucky coincidence.'

In answer, Bastien reached down to close a hand over hers and used that connection to literally lift her upright out of her chair. 'Thanks for looking after her for me, Ciro. We're heading home now.'

'You're making me feel like I shouldn't have gone out,' she whispered thinly as he walked her away.

'No, what you shouldn't have done is flirt with Ciro,' Bastien told her drily.

'I wasn't *flirting* with him!' Lilah snapped back in irate protest, practically running to keep up with his long stride as, with one strong hand gripping hers, he cut through the clumps of pedestrians and dragged her in his wake. It didn't help that almost two glasses of wine had left her head swimming a little...

'He should know better than to get that close to a woman who's mine,' Bastien added grittily, hanging on to his temper by a hair's breadth and ready to grab her up into his arms and bodily carry her back to the car at the first sign of rebellion.

'I'm *not* yours!' Lilah fired back at him with ringing vehemence. 'I simply agreed to sleep with you until you got bored...that's all!'

As that startling statement rang out, Bastien watched curious heads swivel in their direction and compressed his sensual mouth. 'You're shouting.

Would you like a megaphone to share that confession further afield?' he demanded in a tone of incredulous reproof.

'I wasn't shouting,' Lilah hissed with a furious little shrug of her slight shoulders, her bright blue eyes remaining defiant. 'I was merely pointing out the basic terms of our agreement. It was a devil's bargain but I've stuck to *my* side of it. The least I deserve from you in return is respect and consideration.'

'When do *I* qualify for some respect?' Bastien enquired with honeyed scorn.

'When you do something *worthy* of respect,' Lilah slammed back without hesitation.

Unlocking the Ferrari, Bastien scooped Delilah up and stowed her in the passenger seat, impervious to her vocal complaints. He wanted to shout at her. For the first time since his childhood, anger and frustration had reached a peak inside him and he actually wanted to shout. Evidently Delilah really was toxic for him, challenging his self-discipline and making him react in unnervingly abnormal ways.

'And why are you dragging me back to the chateau anyway?' Lilah queried truculently as he swung in bedside her. 'You should be avoiding me like the plague right now.'

In slow motion, Bastien twined his fingers slowly into her long black hair to turn her face up while his other hand framed a delicate cheekbone to hold her steady. The crash of his mouth down on hers felt as inevitable to him as the drowning heat of the summer sun in the sky.

Lilah jerked, as if he had stamped her with a burning brand. Her hand rose of its own volition and delved into his luxuriant black hair, fingertips roaming blissfully over his well-shaped skull. Hunger coursed through her like a hot river of lava, scorching and setting her alight wherever it touched.

She had never felt hunger like it. In fact, it was as if Bastien's lovemaking the night before had released some dam of response inside her that could no longer be suppressed. The resulting ache between her legs and the sheer longing to be intimately touched physically hurt.

Long fingers eased below the hem of her dress and roamed boldly higher.

In a sudden movement Lilah pulled back and slapped her hand down on top of Bastien's to prevent him from conducting a more intimate exploration. '*No,*' she told him shakily.

Bastien swore long and low in Greek, the pulsing at his groin downright painful. He wanted to yank her out of the car, splay her across the bonnet and sink into her hard and fast. He gritted his teeth, rammed home his seat belt and drove out onto the narrow twisting road that snaked down the mountain.

The screaming tension inside the car made Lilah's mouth run dry. It was his own fault. He should never have touched her, she thought piously, pride making her ignore the hollow dissatisfaction of her own body. But then *every* time Bastien touched her he shocked her, she conceded grudgingly, because somehow he always made her desperate to rip his clothes off.

Mortified, she dragged her attention from him and stared out of the car, mouth swollen and tingling.

Manos was waiting for Bastien when he returned. Delilah took the opportunity to race upstairs.

Bastien did not want an audience as he learned that preliminary enquiries had revealed damning facts about one of his personal staff. Andreas Theodakis had taken a smoke break that evening in London, and had been seen using his phone out on the balcony. Furthermore, a colleague had volunteered the news that Theodakis was a gambler. Bastien knew then in his gut that in all likelihood Andreas had tipped off the business press about the Dufort Pharmaceuticals deal.

'I should have confirmation for you one way or another by the end of tomorrow,' Manos concluded.

Bastien had a stiff drink and brooded over the information. No way was he saying sorry when Delilah had made such a big deal of him humbling himself. Indeed, he cringed at the prospect.

He dined alone at his desk, burying himself in work—as was his habit when anything bothered him.

A scrabbling noise made him glance up from the screen, and he frowned at Skippy, who must have sneaked in when Stefan had delivered Bastien's meal. The miniature dachshund was engaged in using a briefcase on the floor as a springboard to the chair on the other side of Bastien's desk. Skippy made it up on to the chair and then with a sudden tremendous leap reached the desk top, whereupon he trotted towards Bastien, his long ears flapping, and dropped his squeaky toy beside Bastien's laptop.

With a sigh, Bastien scooped up the dog before it skidded off the desk and broke its legs, and settled it on the floor. Then, lifting the toy with distaste, he flung it—sending Skippy into a race of panting pleasure.

'I will only throw it once,' he warned the animal.

Unable to get back to work, he walked out onto the balcony and groaned out loud as he paced in the warm evening air. His muscles were stiff.

Banishing Skippy, who was showing annoying signs of wanting to follow him, Bastien went down to the basement gym in an effort to work off some of his tension. A marathon swim, followed by a long, violently cathartic session with the punch bag, sent Bastien into the shower.

All he needed was a good night's sleep and a clear head, he told himself urgently when he was tempted to approach Delilah. He did not need or want *her*...

Lilah sat up late in bed, reading, and fell asleep with the light on, wakening disorientated at around three in the morning. On her way back from the bathroom she thought she heard someone cry out, and she went to the window and brushed back the curtain to look down at the moonlit garden below. Nothing stirred... not even the shadows.

When the sound came again she realised that it had come from Bastien's room, and she crossed the polished wooden floor to listen behind the communicating door with a frown etched between her brows.

The sound of a shout galvanised her into opening the door. Bastien was a dark shape, thrashing about wildly in the bed, and choked cries interspersed with Greek words were breaking from him.

There was no way on earth that Lilah could walk away and leave him suffering like that. He was having a nightmare, that was all, but it was clearly a terrifying one.

She hovered uncertainly by the side of the bed,

and then closed her hand firmly round a sleek tanned muscular shoulder to shake it.

'Wake up, Bastien…it's just a dream,' she told him gently.

CHAPTER EIGHT

ARMS FLAILING AND eyes wild, Bastien reared up and closed a hand round her throat, dragging her down to the bed on top of him as he struggled to focus on her.

'Bastien...it's Lilah!' she gasped, in stricken dismay at the effect of her intervention. 'You were stuck in a bad dream. I was trying to wake you up.'

'Delilah...' Bastien framed dazedly, shifting his tousled dark head in confusion, his eyes glittering dark as night in the faint light emanating from her room. He blinked. 'What are you doing in here?'

'You were having a really bad nightmare,' she repeated as she levered herself away from him and settled on the empty side of the bed. The dampness of perspiration sheened his lean dark features and he was still trembling almost imperceptibly. 'What on earth has got you that worked up?'

'I put my hand round your neck... Did I hurt you?' Bastien demanded, switching on the bedside light and tipping up her chin to examine the faint red fingermarks marring her slender white throat. '*Diavelos*, Delilah... I'm sorry. I could have seriously injured you. You should never have come near me when I was like that. I'm very restless. That's why I always sleep alone.'

'I'm fine… I'm fine… I was worried about you,' she admitted.

'Why the hell would you be worried about a guy who doesn't treat you with respect or consideration?' Bastien prompted grimly.

'I was really concerned about you,' Lilah countered, ignoring that question because she could not have answered it even to her own satisfaction. 'What on earth were you dreaming about?'

His lean dark features were shuttered. 'Believe me, you don't want to know.'

In an abrupt movement that took her by surprise, he pulled her backwards into his arms. Little tremors were still running through his big powerful frame.

Lilah released her breath in a bemused hiss. 'Try to relax,' she urged him, aware of the shattering tension still holding his muscles taut in his big body.

'Don't try to mother me, *glikia mou*,' Bastien growled warningly, resting back against the pillows and breathing in slow and deep before exhaling again. 'That's not what I want from you.'

'Well, you're not getting anything else,' Lilah warned him bluntly.

At that tart response unholy amusement quivered through Bastien's lean, powerful frame and he laughed out loud.

'So, what was the dream about?' she prompted again.

In the low light, Bastien rolled his eyes and laced his fingers round her abdomen as she relaxed back against him. 'I was getting beaten up… It's something that happened when I was a child.'

Taken by surprise, Lilah twisted round in the circle of his arms and lifted her head to look directly at him. 'When you were a *child*?'

'I walked in on my mother, in bed with her drug-dealing boyfriend. She didn't intervene. She was terrified that I would accidentally let it drop to Anatole that she had other men because Anatole paid all our bills.'

Lilah frowned down at him in disbelief. 'For goodness' sake—what age were you?'

He shrugged a broad shoulder. 'Five…six years old? I really don't remember. But I almost died because Athene didn't take me to hospital until the next day—and then not until she had coached me to say that I'd fallen down the stairs.'

'Damaged'—that was how Marielle Durand had labelled Bastien. And for the first time Lilah truly saw that in him, recognising the angry defensive pain in his eyes. His mother had neither wanted nor loved him, and by the sound of it had been a cruel and selfish parent.

Lilah recognised his discomfiture under her continuing scrutiny and she looked away, twisting round to give him back his privacy. Her eyes were smarting with tears, though.

As a teenager she had felt so sorry for herself when her father had been bringing a string of different women home for the night and she'd had to occasionally share the breakfast table with strangers. In retrospect, though, she was realising that she could have suffered much worse experiences, and that no matter how much her father's sex-life had embarrassed her he had always looked after her and loved her.

Bastien had not been so lucky.

'I don't know why I told you that,' Bastien breathed in a harsh undertone.

'Because I'm very persistent when I want to know something,' Lilah declared, with deliberate lightness of tone. 'And because you're shaken up.'

'I don't *get* shaken up,' Bastien asserted predictably.

'Of course not,' Lilah traded, tongue in cheek.

Without warning Bastien sprang off the bed, carting her with him.

'What—?'

'I need a shower,' he ground out.

'I'll go back to—'

'You're not going anywhere,' Bastien contradicted, striding into the en-suite bathroom and straight into the spacious shower with her still in his arms.

'Bastien…what on earth…?' she exclaimed in angry disbelief as he elbowed a button and warm water cascaded down on her from all directions, instantly plastering the nightdress she wore to her body.

Bastien knew he was acting like a mad man, but he was on automatic pilot and he didn't care—because his hunger for Delilah at that moment was overwhelming. He hauled her dripping body up against him and closed his mouth hungrily to the luscious soft pink enticement of hers, long fingers stroking her wet hair back from her face.

Lilah's hands closed over his broad shoulders, clenching there to steady herself as the hot, demanding intensity of the kiss took her by storm. His tongue delved deep into the moist interior of her mouth, plundering a response from her.

She recognised the force of his need, suspecting that Bastien was not in control the way he usually was. Rather than dismaying her, that suspicion excited her beyond bearing—because Bastien was generally so controlled that he unnerved her. In fact, the unashamed passion he was unleashing now was much more to Lilah's taste, and it went to her head even more strongly than the wine that afternoon.

Her hands skimmed down over his lean, strong torso. She could feel the hard urgency of his erection against her midriff, and before she could even let herself think about what she was about to do she had dropped to her knees. The warm water teemed down, somehow separating her from the world and from all the anxious self-judgement that kept her from experimenting. For the first time ever she felt free to do simply as she liked. As she liked and as she wanted. And she was proud of that inner spur of passion for the first time.

Slender fingers roved up over Bastien's hair-roughened muscular thighs, and she was smiling at his sudden ferocious tension as she bent her head—all woman, all feminine power.

Bastien groaned, threw his head back against the tiles and arched his hips to facilitate her, making no attempt to hide his pleasure as she worked magic with her mouth and her tongue and her agile fingers.

His potent reaction gave Lilah a high. For once she was in charge, and what she lacked in experience she more than made up for with creativity and enthusiasm.

Allowing himself to be out of control in any way

was a dark and seductive novelty for Bastien. And when he could no longer withstand the hot, all-encompassing pleasure of her mouth, he bent down and hauled her up to him, bracing her against the tiles as he hitched up her nightdress and clamped her slim thighs to his waist. He plunged into the glorious tight wet heat of her body with a raw groan of masculine pleasure.

Still tender from her first experience the night before, Lilah felt every inch of Bastien's smooth hard length as he surged inside her. Her arms wrapped round his neck for support, her head falling back as he withdrew and surged deep again. Excitement engulfed her in a heady rush, her heart slamming inside her chest, her breath hitching and breaking in her throat.

So sensitive was she that as Bastien increased the tempo and hammered into her the pleasure swelled to an almost painful intensity. The rising heat within her finally soothed the hollow ache of tormenting hunger, and she gasped and moaned in delight. Her hips writhed against the cold tiles as she reached a climax too powerful to restrain and it swept her over the edge, sending intoxicating explosions of blissful sensation rippling through her quivering length as she sagged in Bastien's powerful hold.

By the time she had floated down from that dizzy peak of satisfaction Bastien was trailing off her sodden nightdress and wrapping her in a towel.

'You didn't say sorry...this wasn't supposed to happen between us...' Lilah mumbled in limp reminder as she reclaimed her wits.

'I jumped to conclusions. I was wrong. It appears that one of my staff *was* responsible for the leak to the press,' Bastien shared with taut reluctance as he grabbed up another towel to fold it round her dripping hair.

'Told you so,' Lilah remarked ungraciously.

'I lost my temper with you. I don't *do* that,' Bastien growled half under his breath in explanation. 'When anger is in control, mistakes are made.'

'So you're saying sorry?' Lilah whispered, weak as a kitten as he laid her down on the soft firmness of his bed and pulled a sheet over her cooling skin.

Bastien didn't answer. He didn't do apologies, but he was quite happy for her to assume that he had apologised. He was intent on her, still worked up in an unsettling way he didn't understand. She made him feel alive, crazily *alive*, and for some reason he hadn't had enough of her yet. One taste of her had only made him hunger for more.

He framed her face with long dark fingers, rejoicing in the silky softness of her skin and the rosy purity of her features. He savoured her swollen pink mouth with his own, revelling in the taste of her and the thundering race of his heartbeat as the hunger raged through him again like a tempest.

Bastien kissed with the same wild potency with which he made love, Lilah reflected dizzily, and the pulse of heat was awakening in her pelvis again as his tongue tangled with hers and flicked the ultra-sensitive roof of her mouth in a teasing assault that made her push up against him. Desire shimmied through her like an electrical storm, lighting up every place he touched, from the peaks of her straining nipples to the infinitely delicate damp flesh between her thighs.

'I still want you, *glikia mou*,' Bastien grated, and his stunning dark golden eyes were bright with lingering wonder at that anomaly as he ran his mouth down hungrily over the sweet mounds of her small breasts, licking and tasting and nipping to make her slim body writhe frantically.

As he reached the heart of her arousal and dallied to torment her with every carnal caress he had ever learned she gasped his name over and over again, and he very much liked the sound of his own name on her lips.

Lilah had not believed he could make her want him again so soon, when her body was still heavy with fulfilment, but somehow he'd pushed her to the raw, biting edge of feverish need again, and the first plunge of his powerful male heat inside her felt gloriously necessary.

Her spine arched, wild torrents of joyous sensation cascading through her quivering body as he pushed back her thighs and rose over her, pounding into her tight depths with driving hunger. She thrashed under him, every nerve-ending electrified by the pagan rhythm of his hard thrusts and the inexorable climb towards another climax. When it came, she hit a peak and shattered like glass, shocked by the white-hot intensity of excitement exploding inside her.

She fell back against the pillows, utterly drained of energy, while Bastien groaned long and low and shuddered with pleasure.

Bastien drank in the scent of Delilah's shampoo as he struggled to get his breath back. Her silky hair had the sweet fresh perfume of a summer meadow. Her arms were still wrapped around him and he lifted his tousled dark head to drop a brief but appreciative kiss on her brow.

'You're an unbeatable cure for a nightmare, *glikia mou*,' he husked with wicked amusement, rolling free of her to head for the bathroom.

The minute he arrived there he realised too late what was missing. He had not used a condom—not that last time or the time before it in the shower.

It was a very dangerous oversight that chilled Bastien and made him want to punch something hard in angry self-loathing. The shower beat down on him while some of the worst memories of his life engulfed him and he shuddered, knowing what he must do, knowing that this time around he would not dare to walk away and simply hope for the best.

Delilah needed to know that, whatever happened, her future and that of any child she had would be totally secure.

A towel knotted round his lean brown hips, he strode back into the bedroom and proceeded to disconcert Lilah with what she deemed to be inappropriate questions.

'Why on earth are you asking me such things?' she demanded tautly, her colour high from embarrassment.

'We've had sex twice without a condom,' Bastien told her grimly. 'I'm regularly tested and I'm clean, so there is no risk of an infection. I'm merely trying to calculate the odds of conception.'

Lilah's whole body turned cold at the threat of an unplanned pregnancy. She hadn't noticed the lack of contraception—had been as lost in passion as he must have been. That acknowledgement stung, because she knew how important it was to take precautions and protect herself from such consequences.

Ashamed that she could have been so reckless and immature as to overlook such necessities, she answered his questions about her menstrual cycle and watched his frown steadily darken.

'Obviously you could conceive. You're young, fertile...naturally there's a good chance.' His beautiful mouth compressed hard. 'We'll get married as soon as I can get it organised.'

'*Married?*' Lilah parrotted in a strangled shriek, sitting up in bed with a sudden jerk, her eyes awash with disbelief as she stared back at him.

His unfathomable dark eyes glittered. 'You need to know that whatever happens I'm there for you, and a wedding ring is the only security a man can offer a woman in that situation.'

'People don't rush off and get married simply because of a contraceptive oversight,' Lilah whispered shakily. 'That would be crazy.'

'I know exactly what I'm doing. My first child was aborted when I was only twenty-one,' Bastien explained, shattering her with that flat statement of fact. 'I refuse to risk a repeat of that experience.'

Lilah was poleaxed. 'But...but I—'

'So we'll get married. And if it transpires that we have no reason to *stay* married we'll get an equally quick divorce,' Bastien assured her smoothly, as though such a fast turnaround from marriage to divorce would be the most natural development in the world.

'But we can't just get married on the off-chance that I might be pregnant,' she muttered incredulously.

'If you have conceived we'll be married and you'll be less tempted to consider a termination,' Bastien pointed out with assurance. 'We don't need to publicise our marriage in the short term, or drag anyone else into our predicament. We'll have a private wedding.'

Stunned, Lilah flopped down flat again, exhaustion rolling over her like a hefty blanket. It was all too much to take in. The shocking revelations of his past and the sheer impossibility of their future.

'We'll argue about it in the morning,' she countered in a daze. 'You're thinking worst-case scenario.'

'No, I've already *lived* the worst-case scenario,' Bastien contradicted with an edge of derision. 'And that was losing the child I wanted because the woman concerned decided that she didn't.'

Lilah winced, recognising the edge of bitterness in his dark deep drawl. She wondered who that woman had been, while marvelling at how much Bastien was revealing about himself. He had a deep, sensitive side to his nature that astonished her. For the first time she wondered what it had felt like for him—a man who wanted a child with a woman when the woman did not feel the same. Her heart ached for him. Clearly he had grieved that loss, but he had also interpreted the termination as a personal rejection and a humiliation, which struck her as even more sad.

Without comment she watched him stride lithely back to his own room, utterly unconcerned by his nudity. But why would he be concerned? an inner voice asked. When you were *that* perfectly built and physically beautiful you had to be aware of the fact.

She stretched out in the big bed, wondering why

she wished he had stayed…wondering why what he had told her had left her feeling bereft and unsettled.

Had he loved the woman who had chosen not to have his child? Why did it bother her that Bastien might once have cared deeply for another woman? Evidently back then Bastien had not been quite as emotionally detached and untouchable as he was now. He had cared…he had been hurt. Why did that touch something deep down inside her and wound her? It couldn't be jealousy… It couldn't possibly be jealousy.

She didn't care about Bastien in the smallest way, Lilah assured herself agitatedly. Bastien Zikos was simply the man she'd slept with to fulfil her side of their agreement to be his mistress. That was all he wanted from her. And all she had ever wanted from him was that he reopen the factory and re-employ her father.

Honesty urged Lilah to admit that she *was* lying to herself. Two years earlier, when she had first met Bastien, she had very quickly begun developing deep feelings for him—but his sole reaction to *her* had been superficial and sexual. And nothing had changed since then, she reminded herself doggedly. Even if she was pregnant—even if she agreed to marry him—nothing would change between them. If she hadn't got to Bastien on a more meaningful level when they first met it was extremely unlikely that anything more would develop the second time around.

But how dared he simply assume that if she had conceived she would automatically want to consider a termination? He had no right to make that assumption—no right to try and take control of that decision either.

Too tired to lie awake agonising about what might never happen, Lilah ultimately dropped off to sleep.

The next morning that entire conversation with Bastien about getting married seemed surreal to Lilah. She was still deep in her bemused thoughts when she went downstairs for breakfast.

Bastien watched Delilah cross the terrace, a lithe, slim figure in a turquoise playsuit that showcased her tiny waist and long slim legs. She looked very young, with her black curls rippling loose round her shoulders. He watched her sit down and settle anxious sapphire-blue eyes on him.

Clad in tailored cream chinos and a black T-shirt, Bastien was casually seated on the low wall bounding the terrace, with a cup of coffee in his hand. His bronzed sculpted features smooth shaven, his lean, powerful body fluidly relaxed, he exuded poise, sophistication and an absolute charisma which stole Lilah's breath from her lungs.

A tiny muscle low in her pelvis clenched and her face coloured hotly as she became uncomfortably aware of the damp flesh between her thighs.

'I've been thinking, and I believe you're worrying about something that's unlikely to happen. It's not always that easy to get pregnant,' Lilah told Bastien quietly, keen to distract him from looking at her too closely because Bastien was far too astute at reading women. 'It took my stepmother months to conceive.'

'I'm not about to change my mind about marriage as a solution, Delilah,' Bastien warned her, secretly amused and impressed that she lacked the avaricious streak that would have made many women grab at the chance to marry him. 'While the arrangements are being made—there's a lot of paperwork involved in getting married in France—we'll continue here as normal. My lawyers are drawing up a pre-nup as we speak—'

Lilah poured her tea and groaned. 'You're really serious about this…'

'It may not seem immediately obvious to you in our current relationship,' Bastien remarked in a roughened undertone, watching her nibble at a croissant with unconscious sensuality and gritting his teeth as he hardened in response, 'but if you do prove to be pregnant I have a lot to offer as a husband and a father…'

Who was she? Lilah immediately wanted to know. Who was the evil witch who had made Bastien feel worthless at the age of twenty-one when he had been little more than a boy?

'I know that, Bastien,' she said quietly. 'Who was the woman who had the termination?'

Bastien grimaced. 'This long after the event, there is no need for us to discuss that.'

Lilah tilted her chin. 'If you want me to marry you in these circumstances I have a right to know the whole story.'

'Her name is Marina Kouros. She's the daughter of a wealthy businessman.'

'Greek?'

'Yes. She hung out with my half-brother, Leo. I knew she had a thing for him, but he saw her only as a friend.'

Lilah winced when he described that connection. 'Complicated…'

'Nothing I couldn't handle at the time, I thought.

I was very confident with women even at that age,' Bastien admitted bleakly. '*Too* confident, as it turned out. Of course I was infatuated with Marina. We had a one-night stand but I wanted more. I didn't see it at the time, but she was using me to try and make Leo sit up and take notice of her.'

'You were *brothers*. It was wrong of her to come between you like that,' Lilah opined.

'To be fair, Marina didn't intend to cause trouble, and Leo and I have never been close. I also know why she went for the termination behind my back,' he admitted tautly. 'I was illegitimate and penniless—hardly a winning package for a wealthy socialite. Unfortunately when Leo heard the rumours that I had got her pregnant she lied to save face with him and pretended that I had bullied her into the abortion clinic. He's held that against me ever since.'

'That's *so* unfair,' Lilah breathed angrily.

Bastien shrugged a broad shoulder. 'Very little in my life has been fair,' he derided softly. 'That's why I prefer to make my own luck and my own fortune. I don't owe anyone anything and that's how I like it, *glikia mou*.'

'But *I* would prefer not to risk having an unnecessary marriage and divorce in my relationship history,' Lilah told him quietly. 'I think we should wait and see if we have anything to worry about first.'

His dark golden eyes hardened. 'Not this time.'

'Even if I have conceived I don't think I'd choose a termination,' Lilah added.

Bastien sprang upright and set down his coffee cup, an aggressive edge to his movements. 'We'll do this my way. We'll get married.'

Lilah stood up. 'It's not the course of action I would choose, Bastien.'

'I don't care. This is an amendment to our original agreement,' he declared without hesitation. 'Deal with it.'

Lilah turned away from him, angry and stressed.

'You'll have a few days to think your position over,' Bastien told her. 'I have to make a trip to Asia, to check out some trouble at one of my manufacturing plants.'

Taken aback, Lilah turned. 'How long will you be away?'

'About a week.'

Lilah had a second cup of tea while Bastien talked on the phone in a foreign language. *Deal with it*, he had told her. An amendment to their original agreement? Was he *threatening* her? Would continuing refusal to marry him on her part be treated as a breach of that agreement? Did she dare push it?

What, after all, *was* she planning to do should Bastien's fears prove correct and she found herself pregnant? Her skin turned clammy with anxiety. If she was pregnant she would want Bastien's support every step of the way, she reflected ruefully. Maybe, just maybe, she was fighting the wrong battle...

CHAPTER NINE

IT WAS A beautiful dress. Exquisitely simple in shape, it flattered Lilah's slender figure, with long tight lace sleeves, a boat-shaped neckline and a slimline skirt. Her wedding gown, she acknowledged in lingering astonishment as she studied her reflection. It was her wedding day, and she still couldn't believe that she was actually about to marry Bastien Zikos.

The whole of the previous week had been taken up with marriage-orientated activity. Accompanied by one of Bastien's personal assistants, a fluent French-speaker, she had undergone an interview at the local *mairie*—the mayor's office, where the ceremony would take place. A whole heap of personal documents had been certified and presented on her behalf to fulfil the legal requirements, and forty-eight hours later, following a meeting with a lawyer at the chateau to protect her interests, she had signed a pre-nuptial agreement. Bastien had made liberal provision for her in the event of a divorce, offering a far more generous settlement than she thought necessary.

'Look on it as compensation,' Bastien had advised her on the phone, when she had protested the size of that settlement. 'You didn't want to marry me, but you're doing it.'

It wouldn't be a *real* marriage, she told herself soothingly as she clasped the diamond pendant round her throat. And wasn't that just as well? Bastien had been away for seven days and she had missed him almost from the moment of his departure. How was that possible? How could she miss the male she had believed she hated, who had persuaded her into a morally indefensible sexual relationship?

Lilah walked to the window and breathed in slow and deep, struggling to calm herself. She had *not* become attached to Bastien, and she had *not* fallen for him. She was just wildly attracted to him. She had also begun to understand him better as she'd come to appreciate his tough childhood and the experiences which had made him the hard, aggressive character that he was.

She wasn't *excusing* anything he had done, was she? No—she remained fully aware of Bastien's every flaw, and was therefore completely safe from getting attached to him, she assured herself soothingly.

A knock sounded on the bedroom door. It was time for her to leave. Manos smiled at her as she emerged from the room, rich fabric gliding in silken folds round her legs. Bastien had had a whole rack of designer wedding gowns sent to her and she had been taken aback, having assumed that they would be bypassing all such frills.

'No, this should look like a normal wedding,' Bastien had decreed.

Yet how could it look or feel normal when neither of them had any family members present?

Lilah felt absurdly guilty that she was about to get married without her father's knowledge.

Bastien was waiting in the hall. Clad in a superbly tailored pale grey suit, he looked breathtakingly handsome. When she met his long-lashed dark golden eyes her heart thudded and her pulses quickened, and she could feel heat rushing into her cheeks.

'You look fantastic,' he husked, closing a hand over hers as she reached the bottom step.

'When did you get back?'

'At dawn. I slept during the flight,' he shared, just as Stefan presented Lilah with a small bunch of flowers and she thanked him warmly.

They came to a halt in the stone front doorway as a photographer stepped forward to capture them on film.

'I wasn't expecting him,' Lilah admitted out of the corner of her mouth.

'This is not a moment we can easily recapture,' Bastien declared.

'But who's going to be interested?' she whispered helplessly.

'Our child will be interested in our wedding day,' Bastien countered.

'But…' Her lips clamped shut on a rush of denial as the photographer asked her to relax and smile.

She was convinced that there wasn't going to be a pregnancy, or a child, but she could see that Bastien had already decided otherwise.

A limousine whisked them to the *mairie*, a sleepy creamy stone building sited behind the war memorial in a small village. It was a civil ceremony, conducted by a middle-aged female official. Lilah held her breath as Bastien slid a gold ring on to her finger and she performed the same office for him, albeit more clumsily, all fingers and thumbs in her extreme self-consciousness as she thought about what the gesture actually meant: Bastien was her husband now.

When they emerged back into the sunshine the photographer was waiting, and she laughed and smiled, suddenly grateful that the unsettling ceremony was over and she could forget about it.

She was climbing back into the limo when a sports car shot to a sudden halt at the other side of the road and a woman called, *'Bastien?'*

Bastien stepped back from the limo and swung round as a lithe blonde scrambled out of the sports car and ran to greet him. She wore only a chiffon wrap, which was split to the waist at either side to show off her fabulous legs and brief leopard print bikini pants.

Lilah smoothed her gown over her knees and watched as the blonde kissed Bastien on both cheeks and he returned the greeting. The woman chattered, her slim hands moving expressively in the air. Very French, very chic, Lilah conceded, deliberately looking away from the encounter. Bastien's dealings with other women were none of her business.

Her tummy flipped, her chin coming up. No, that couldn't be true *or* acceptable. She was Bastien's wife now, and that had to make a difference.

'Who is she?' Lilah enquired when Bastien finally joined her and the limo moved off again.

'Chantal Baudin—one of my neighbours,' Bastien divulged carelessly.

'You've slept with her…haven't you?'

The instant those provocative words leapt off Lilah's tongue she was shocked by them, because she hadn't even known that that question was in her head.

'On several occasions over the years since I bought the chateau,' Bastien revealed, as cool as ice water in tone. 'She's a model.'

'What else would she be?' Lilah traded drily, while colour flared over her cheekbones like a revealing banner, because she felt as though an evil genie had taken over both her brain *and* her tongue.

'We were ships-that-pass-casual,' Bastien qualified very quietly. 'Not that that's any of your business.'

Lilah's shot a stubborn look at him, sapphire-blue eyes bright and defiant. 'Oh, it's my business *now*,' she assured him without hesitation. 'For as long as you remain married to me you have to be a one-woman man.'

A line of colour flared over Bastien's exotic cheekbones and his dark golden eyes smouldered. 'That sounds suspiciously like a warning.'

'It was. Do you expect *me* to stay away from other men?' Lilah asked dangerously.

'Of course,' Bastien breathed, in a harsh uncompromising undertone.

'Well, let's not be sexist about it—the rule cuts both ways. While we're married, your wings are clipped,' Lilah pronounced with satisfaction.

'Presumably you intend to ensure that the sacrifice of my sexual freedom is worth my while?' Bastien purred, black lashes dropping low over his gaze.

Lilah clashed with expectant dark eyes, brilliant as stars in a black sky, and her tummy performed a somersault while damp heat gathered at her feminine core. She shifted uneasily on the seat, uncomfortable with the potent physical effect Bastien had on her. Even when he annoyed her he could still make her want him. One glance at those high cheekbones and those stunning eyes and she melted into a puddle of longing.

Lunch awaited them on their return to the chateau. The table had been set with white linen, lace and rose petals, and Lilah stiffened in dismay when she saw it because it was very bridal and romantic. But the meal was superb, and Bastien's businesslike account of how he had dealt with the problems at his Asian manufacturing plant relaxed Lilah again.

Bastien studied Delilah, ultra-feminine and lovely, in a dress that merely enhanced her petite proportions, wondering if she was pregnant. He wanted a child, he acknowledged. Perhaps it was simply that he was *ready* for a child and for a change in lifestyle. But would he have felt that way with any woman other than Delilah?

'I should get changed,' Lilah murmured over coffee.

'*I* want to take off that dress.'

Lilah coloured. 'It's the middle of the day, Bastien.'

'My libido is not controlled by the clock. In any case, we're newly married and anything goes,' Bastien pointed out smoothly as he rose from his chair.

But Lilah refused to think of them as a married couple, thinking it wiser to regard their current relationship as simply an extension of their original arrangement. In other words, barring the ring on her wedding finger, she was still Bastien's mistress and his desired entertainment between the sheets. It would be very unwise, she thought, to start thinking of herself as occupying any more important or permanent role in Bastien's life.

Lean brown fingers closed over hers and she walked upstairs with him, her slender body taut with anticipation. She listened to the faint buzz of his mobile receiving messages and suppressed a sigh. Bastien never, ever switched his phone off, and it set her teeth on edge.

Bastien glanced at his phone and frowned when he saw the text. Chantal was making a nuisance of herself. He had told her that he was not alone at the chateau and she should have taken the hint that he wasn't available. Perhaps he should have mentioned that he had just got married, but why telegraph that news when there might be no need to do so? After all, if Delilah *hadn't* conceived he would soon be alone and free as a bird again, he reminded himself. And that was what he wanted, wasn't it? What he had always wanted: freedom without rules or ties.

Obviously he still had to get Delilah out of his system. Surely one more week would do that? Although he grudgingly admitted to himself that he did not *like* the prospect of parting with her. Why did the thought feel like a threat?

And then the sure knowledge hit him like a bombshell, blowing apart everything he had believed he knew about himself. He didn't *want* to let Delilah go. He wanted to *keep* her.

Struggling to rationalise that aberrant urge, he ran down the zip on her dress very slowly and eased her smoothly out of its concealing folds. Her porcelain-pale skin showed to advantage against the defiantly unconventional scarlet bra and panties she sported.

For some reason he had expected to find her wearing blue underpinnings, in line with that old bridal rhyme about something old, something new. He scanned her slender legs, but there was no garter to be seen either.

'Something blue?' he queried.

'It wasn't a real wedding, so I didn't see the point of bothering with tradition,' Delilah explained cheerfully.

Exasperation and annoyance shot through Bastien, who had assumed that she would be more sentimental. 'It felt real enough to me.'

'It's not real when you've already planned the divorce *before* you get married,' Delilah told him with vehement conviction.

'No man of my wealth marries without a pre-nup. And I won't be divorcing you if you're carrying my child,' Bastien pointed out, lifting her up to seat her at the foot of the bed, while wishing she would stop talking about divorce.

'I just don't think that it's very likely...that I'll be pregnant,' she extended, feeling insanely bare in her flimsy underwear while he remained fully dressed.

'Time will tell,' Bastien traded, easing off her silk sandals. 'And I do have an entire week to concentrate on getting you pregnant.'

Her bright blue eyes flew wide. 'What on earth do you mean?'

'Now that we're married it would be silly to start taking precautions again,' Bastien pronounced.

'Not to *my* way of thinking. If there is a decision still to be made on that score I don't think I want to *plan* to have a baby with a womaniser,' Lilah told him tartly.

Bastien shrugged free of his jacket and pitched it on to a chair before tugging at his tie. Whatever it took, he was determined to keep her. 'If you give me a baby I can promise that you'll be the only woman in my life.'

Lilah was hugely disconcerted by that offer, coming at her out of nowhere. 'You want a baby that much?'

But only with *her*, Bastien completed inwardly. She had first-rate qualities which he had noticed from the first. She wasn't greedy, dishonest or manipulative, like so many of the women he had known. In addition she was loyal, and kind to those she cared about, and she was a curiously attractive combination of downright old-fashioned sensible and mulishly spirited. Add in her looks and sex appeal and Delilah Moore-Zikos inhabited a class all of her own...

Not that he was planning to share that high opinion with her, though. Particularly not when she talked as though she was indifferent to both him and the prospect of a baby. But he didn't believe that. Like him, Delilah tended to hold back, judging a situation before she bared her soul or committed to a path of action.

Having reached his decision at a speed which slightly stunned him, Bastien curved long fingers to her slim shoulders. 'I want a baby with *you*.'

'But that pre-nup—'

'*Thee mou*...think outside the box,' he urged. 'I will settle down with you if you give me a child.'

Lilah went pink. 'And why would you think that I would be interested in *that* outcome?'

Bastien elevated an ebony brow. 'Aren't you?'

'Are we bargaining again, Bastien?'

Lilah was so tense she could hardly breathe. The unthinkable was happening: Bastien Zikos, the legendary womaniser, was offering her fidelity and a real marriage.

'Negotiating?' he countered.

'I may not even be able to *get* pregnant,' Lilah countered with quiet practicality.

'If and when that happens we'll deal with it, *glikia mou*,' Bastien told her levelly. 'I don't expect an easy ride. Nothing worthwhile is ever easy.'

Her heart swelled like a balloon inside her chest at that forthright opinion, which perfectly matched her own. Tears lashed the back of her eyes and she blinked them back furiously to focus on the beautiful burnished golden shimmer of his gaze.

'In that case, I'll… I'll give it a go,' she responded jerkily, afraid of the way she was laying herself open to getting hurt again, but desperately wanting to give him another chance.

Another chance to smash her heart to smithereens? Another chance to walk away from her without a backward glance and console himself with other women? How likely was it that Bastien could settle down into marriage? Did she dare risk bringing a child into so potentially volatile a relationship? And why was she even considering doing so?

Stealing a glance at his lean, darkly handsome face, she felt her breath hitch in her throat. The freedom of choice was suddenly cruelly wrenched from her, along with much of her pride. The reason she so badly wanted to give Bastien another chance was that she had fallen hard for him two years earlier and had struggled to fight feelings almost stronger than she was. Sadly, now that she was actually in Bastien's life and wearing his ring on her finger, she was weaker, more open to hope and dream fulfilment and love.

And that was the most basic truth, which she could no longer ignore or deny. She *loved* Bastien Zikos— had fallen like a giant stone the very first time he had settled those gorgeous dark eyes on her and smiled.

'You look so serious,' Bastien censured as he trailed off his shirt to reveal the torso that starred in her every fantasy. He was so wonderfully well-built, and he worked at staying fit—a reality etched in the lean hard sheet of roped muscle framing his pectoral muscles and abdomen.

Lilah's mouth ran dry. He brought his mouth down on hers, nibbling sexily at her full lower lip, swiping the upper with the tip of his tongue to gain entry to the intimate space beyond. A ball of heat mushroomed inside her when his tongue flicked against her own. Her hands spread on his chest, fingertips grazing hair-roughened skin and smoothing down to feel him jerk with sensitivity when she found the hard thrusting length of him.

With a hungry groan he lifted her up and brought her down again on the bed, arranging her over him with careful hands.

'I want you,' Bastien growled, dark eyes shooting golden sparks over her warmly flushed face.

'You sound so aggressive,' Lilah scolded as she obediently bent forward for him to unclasp her bra.

'It's been a week.' He swore bitterly. 'An endless, frustrating week.'

Strong hands pulled her down to him, to enable

him to close his lips round a pouting pink nipple. He hauled her close to him and rolled her over.

'Didn't *think* I was going to get to stay on top,' Lilah muttered with helpless bite.

His broad chest rumbled with amusement. 'Some day very soon…but not today,' he agreed in a roughened undertone.

Employing every sensual skill he had acquired, Bastien worked his way down over Delilah's slim squirming body, revelling in each sound that revealed her enjoyment. As her hips bucked in climax and she cried his name he smiled and flipped her over, lifting her up on to her knees.

He slid against her damp flesh to tease her, and then when she complained in frustration he sank into her, hard and deep.

Lilah moaned, her head still swimming and her body still sensitised, floating on the aftermath of extreme pleasure. Extraordinarily conscious of Bastien's every slight movement, Lilah felt her heart race and her pulse quicken with exhilaration. Intense excitement controlled her as he ground his hips into hers, quickening his pace until all she was conscious of was the wild, feverish climb of pleasure. As the ascent to satisfaction consumed her spasms of potent sensation coursed through her quivering body and then rose to an irresistible peak, leaving her thrashing in explosive convulsions of delight.

'I'll never move again,' she whispered limply in the aftermath.

'I'll move you,' Bastien husked, turning her round in the circle of his arms, his breath fanning her cheek, his body hot and damp against hers.

The scent of his skin enveloped her and she smiled up at him.

'I do hope you appreciate that you're not getting out of this bed for the rest of the day?' Bastien purred. 'But I'll make up for it tomorrow. I'm taking the rest of the week off. You will have my full attention, *kardoula mou*.'

Lilah rubbed her face against a broad brown shoulder, gloriously relaxed and feeling amazingly happy. She loved him, and he was with her, and his entire attention was on her. For the moment that was enough. And for the first time she didn't feel like Bastien's mistress—she felt like his wife, and it felt good.

A week after their wedding day Lilah woke suddenly during the night to register that Bastien had got out of bed and was pacing naked while he spoke Greek into his phone, his lean strong features stressed and taut. He waved a hand to silence her when she mouthed a query and she had to be patient, even though she didn't *feel* patient, lying back against the pillows and wondering what had happened to put that look of concern on his beautiful face.

So much had changed between them in the course of a week. Bastien had let down some of his barriers and was sharing a bed with her every night. Only once had he had another bad dream, and wakening to find her leaning over him had put more exciting pursuits into his mind, she recalled, her body heating at that wickedly erotic memory.

By day they had explored the chateau grounds before ranging further afield. They had gone to a jazz concert in the vineyards near Vaison-Ventoux-en-

Provence. They had strolled round vibrant markets, walked through narrow cobbled streets to enjoy coffee in shaded squares with softly flowing fountains. The hilltop villages were wonderfully picturesque, and the views spectacular.

He had bought her a gorgeous leather handbag in a workshop, and laughed heartily at the colourful pottery hen she had bought for Vickie, questioning that she could really *like* her stepmother and still buy her such a thing.

On several evenings they had dined out in local restaurants, although truthfully they had yet to eat anywhere that could compete with the superb food Marie served at the chateau. Some nights they made love until dawn…some afternoons they didn't get out of bed until the need to eat drove them out. His insatiable hunger for her was mercifully matched by hers for him, and with his encouragement Lilah had become more adventurous.

The only little niggle at the back of her mind, that had prevented her from totally relaxing, was the question of how Bastien was likely to react if she *didn't* prove to be pregnant. After all, was it really her he wanted, or was he merely giving way to a long-suppressed desire to become a father?

He could become a father with almost any woman, couldn't he? Lilah didn't like to think that her being in the right place at the right time was all that had prompted Bastien to seek a more lasting relationship with *her*. In any case, in another few days she would know whether or not she had conceived. And even if she had it was perfectly possible that she would still never tell Bastien that she loved him for fear of making him feel trapped, she thought ruefully.

'What's wrong?' she asked as Bastien cast aside his phone and paced restively back across the room.

'That was my brother, Leo,' he explained grimly. 'My father's in hospital in Athens with a suspected heart attack. Leo says there's no need for me to go, because he'll keep me posted, but...'

'Naturally you want to be there,' Lilah slotted in.

'But equally naturally Leo and his mother don't want me there.'

'How is *that* natural?' Lilah pressed, immediately defensive on Bastien's behalf. 'Anatole is as much your father as your brother's.'

'I may have lived with my father's family for years, but I was never part of that family,' Bastien pointed out drily. 'I'm never a welcome visitor. Leo's mother Cleta—my father's wife—hates me.'

Lilah compressed her lips. 'After the number of years that have passed since your mother's death, and the years you lived in her home with Anatole, that's very definitely *her* problem—not yours,' she pronounced with conviction. 'Don't let *anyone* make you feel as though you don't have the right to see your own father. You're his son too.'

The fiery gleam that illuminated Bastien's dark eyes only accentuated the worried frown stamped on his lean bronzed face. 'I do want to see him. We'll fly out as soon as I can get it organised.'

CHAPTER TEN

BASTIEN AND LILAH drove straight to the hospital from the airport. Lilah hung back a little as they entered the waiting room, because at first glance it seemed to be filled with people. Anatole was still having tests, and only close family would be allowed to visit him. The target of a slew of stares as she entered the room, Lilah flushed and acknowledged that she might be married to Bastien but she did not *feel* like a member of his family.

A small, curvy older woman, improbably dressed in a purple brocade evening coat and matching dress, and more diamonds than Lilah had ever seen outside a shop window, shot a look of derision at Bastien. 'How *dare* you bring one of your whores to the hospital?' she spat.

The very tall black-haired male standing to one side of this shrew stiffened and said something in Greek, while Bastien curved a strong arm to Lilah's tense spine.

'May I introduce my wife, Delilah? This is Cleta Zikos, my father's wife...and my brother Leo and his wife, Grace.'

'Your *wife*?' the pretty redhead exclaimed in an

unmistakable English accent as she surged forward. 'When did you get *married*?'

'Recently,' Lilah responded, grateful that Leo's wife seemed warm and friendly in comparison to his brother, who seemed stunned by the news, and Anatole's sour-faced wife, who had merely grimaced, making it clear that any attachment of Bastien's— married or otherwise—was not welcome.

Annoyance rippled through Lilah at the disturbing awareness that after his mother's death Bastien had spent *years* living in Cleta Zikos's home. Evidently Cleta had never tried to treat Bastien as a stepchild, but had preferred to despise him for the reality that his late mother had been her husband's mistress.

Bastien's brother, Leo, stepped forward to congratulate them. 'Never thought I'd live to see the day,' she heard him quip, half under his breath.

Apart from their similar height and build, the two men did not look obviously related. The awkwardness between them was apparent as they engaged in stilted chat, slipping into Greek, presumably to discuss their father's condition.

Grace settled a hand on Lilah's sleeve and urged her over to some seats at the far wall. 'So, tell all, Delilah,' she urged. 'Leo was convinced that Bastien would stay single for ever.'

'Everyone but Bastien calls me Lilah,' Lilah shared with a rueful look.

'We are both married to very stubborn individuals,' Grace said with a grin. 'Neither one of them gives an inch in a tight corner.'

Lilah glanced up as another woman arrived and

Cleta Zikos rushed up to welcome the tall, shapely brunette with a flood of Greek.

'Who's that?' she asked her companion.

'Marina Kouros—an old friend of the family.'

Bastien's first love, Lilah registered, her heart performing a heavy thud inside her chest.

Clearly Bastien had had good taste, even at the age of twenty-one, because the lively chattering brunette was a classic beauty. She watched Marina stiffen and pale, her animation taking a dip when she belatedly appreciated that Bastien was present. She didn't smile at him and he didn't smile at her. They exchanged a stiff nod of acknowledgement, but Lilah fancied that Bastien looked at his former lover longer than was necessary, and a twist of green jealousy shivered through her.

What was that old cliché about a man never forgetting his first love? Her attention roved down to Marina's hand, which bore no rings, indicating that the woman was still single.

'I propose that you, me and Marina take a break for coffee at our home,' Grace suggested. 'None of us are going to be allowed in to see Anatole anyway. Cleta, I would invite you, but I know you won't leave the hospital until you've seen your husband.'

'I'll pick you up later,' Bastien told Lilah quietly, clearly content for her to depart.

'I'd be happy to stay,' she told him.

His dark golden eyes skimmed her troubled face. 'I don't need support, *hara mou.*'

That was a matter of opinion, Lilah reflected ruefully, avoiding Cleta's haughtily resentful glance and Leo's cool, curious regard. In such company Bastien stood very much alone, and she hated that it was like that for him. But then in such a dysfunctional family circle he had *always* been alone, she thought unhappily. Bastien was still treated like the illegitimate son—the outsider to be resented and kept at a distance.

Not unnaturally, Bastien had eventually learned to live like that—never getting too close to people, steering clear of messy human emotions as best he could because he had seen far too many unpleasant displays of turbulent emotion while he was growing up.

'How do you get on with your mother-in-law?' Lilah asked Grace as the three women stepped into a lift.

'I don't see much of her. Her life revolves round Anatole. She's a bit of a cold fish,' Grace volunteered with a grimace.

Lilah pressed her arm against her breasts. They were sore, aching and tender, but she occasionally suffered from such discomfort before her menstrual cycle kicked in. On the other hand, she was already late… She was planning to do a pregnancy test the following morning, but was convinced it would be a waste of time because she just couldn't imagine that she would be pregnant.

She rested back against the wall of the lift, feeling incredibly weary, and noticed that Marina was staring at her.

'I was surprised to hear that Bastien had got married,' she admitted baldly.

'He rushed me into it,' Lilah responded coolly, studying the woman whose one-night stand with Bastien almost ten years earlier had caused such lasting and damaging repercussions.

'He must've been scared of losing you,' Grace opined.

'Very little scares Bastien,' Lilah said wryly, thinking of how she and Bastien had started out at daggers drawn, and of how quickly her feelings had changed.

Obviously she had no resistance when it came to Bastien. Love had been softening her up for a serious fall from the beginning, she reckoned ruefully, feeling nausea stirring in her tense tummy because she felt so ridiculously uncomfortable in Marina's presence.

Lilah was experiencing a volatile cocktail of jealousy and resentment, and telling herself that she was not entitled to those reactions wasn't helping. She hated knowing that Marina had once shared a bed with Bastien, hated the fact that Bastien had wanted Marina first, and hated even more the reality that Marina could have had him but had instead chosen to throw him away, while at the same time lying about him to poison his relationship with his only sibling.

'You're very quiet,' Grace commented in the limousine.

'I napped during the flight but I'm still very tired,' Lilah confided with an apologetic smile.

'When did you first meet Bastien?' Marina asked.

'Over two years ago.'

'He's quite a guy,' Marina remarked, in a tone that Lilah took exception to because it oozed intimacy to her sensitive hearing. 'A lot of women will envy you.'

Including you? Lilah wondered, thinking that the brunette might well have come to live to regret rejecting Bastien once he had become rich and successful, and as such much more socially acceptable.

It dismayed Lilah that she should feel so angry with Marina and so very protective of Bastien.

Leo and Grace lived in a palatial town house. A nanny brought their daughter, Rosie, to meet them. The toddler was adorable, and Lilah relaxed in little Rosie's presence—but only until she began wondering how Bastien would react to her not being pregnant. After that disappointment would he still want to stay married to her? Or would that single disappointment be sufficient to knock the gloss off his belief that he wanted to keep her as his wife? Rich, powerful men didn't deal generously with disappointments because they met with very few.

A chill ran down Lilah's spine as she sipped her tea and tried to think cheerfully of returning to the life she had left behind.

'I was hoping that you and Bastien would join us for dinner some evening while you're in Athens,' Grace shared. 'Break the ice a bit.'

'I think it would take an ice pick,' Lilah confided ruefully.

'Bastien's not the family type. He's a natural loner,' Marina remarked.

Lilah stiffened angrily and her bright blue eyes sparked. 'Bastien might be closer to his brother if *you* hadn't soured their relationship by lying about what happened between you and Bastien ten years ago,' Lilah condemned, the stream of recrimination racing off her tongue before she could even stop to think about what she was saying.

In response to Lilah's outburst the most appalling

silence spread. Marina had turned the colour of ash, and Grace was staring at Lilah in wide-eyed consternation.

'I... I don't know what to say,' Marina responded, and as a deep flush highlighted her cheeks her guiltiness was obvious to Lilah.

'But I do. Delilah...time for you to leave.'

A deeply unwelcome voice sounded from behind the sofa she was sitting on. Lilah's head swivelled and she focused on Bastien in shock. The fact that he had heard what she had said to Marina was stamped on his lean darkly handsome face and in the threatening golden blaze of his eyes. She had embarrassed him by prying into his past and he was absolutely furious.

Her cheeks warm, she stood up and encountered a sympathetic glance from Grace.

'I'm sorry. I put my foot in it...trod where I shouldn't... whatever you want to call it,' Lilah muttered in a rush as soon as she was in the car with him.

'We'll discuss it when we get back to the apartment.'

'How's your father?' she asked.

'They think he's had a minor heart attack. He's going to have to change his lifestyle—eat less, exercise more,' he breathed curtly. 'Cleta's staying with him. I'll go back to see him later.'

Lilah stole a glance at his grim bronzed profile and cursed the misfortune that had led to Bastien overhearing her attack on his former lover. She knew she was in the wrong. She should have minded her own business. Should never have embarrassed Grace like that in her home. And now Bastien was furious with her.

She gritted her teeth, angry that she had spoken on impulse and without sensible forethought, but not sorry that she had told Marina what she thought of her behaviour.

His apartment was a penthouse, furnished in contemporary style and full of airy space, glass, metal and stone.

Lilah slung her bag down in the main reception room and sat down heavily. 'Say what you have to say,' she urged apprehensively, her nerves worn to a thread by the enforced wait.

Bastien settled burning golden eyes on her. 'What the *hell* got into you? I told you something private and you used it as a weapon to attack Marina. It was none of your business. You embarrassed me and you embarrassed Grace.'

'Well, if I embarrassed Marina, I'm not sorry,' Lilah fired back. 'She deserved what I said. And I didn't specify what I was talking about in any way, so I doubt if I embarrassed anyone.'

'Is that all you've got to say to me?' Bastien raked back at her rawly. 'You dug up something very confidential from my past. I can't *believe* that I even told you now. I should've known a woman couldn't be trusted.'

'Oh, don't throw any of that prejudiced nonsense at me!' Lilah warned him, equally rawly. 'It just got to me when Marina walked in all smiles and charm, acting as if she was a friend of the family.'

'She *is* a friend!'

'Not of yours, she's not!' Lilah flung back feelingly. 'She's caused a whole lot of trouble between you and your brother and you shouldn't have let her lies stand unchallenged. Your pride makes you your own worst enemy, Bastien!'

'I can't believe we're even having this conversation. Nothing that happened between Marina and I or Leo and I is anything to do with you. Where the hell do you get the nerve to interfere?'

'Maybe…just maybe…I was trying to do something for you.'

'You had no right to upset Marina like that.'

'Marina?' Lilah gasped as if he had punched her, because she was suddenly desperately short of breath, pierced to the heart that he should be more concerned about his former lover's feelings than about her.

'Yes—Marina,' Bastien repeated curtly. 'Of *course* she was upset. I saw her face. She knew instantly what you were referring to. You can't have thought this through, Delilah.'

Lilah was wounded by the angle the conversation had taken and fighting to hide the fact from him. Bastien was standing there, all lean, powerful and poised and devastatingly beautiful, and he was defending another woman to her face. He was *her* husband but he wasn't on her side.

Her tummy flipped, leaving her struggling against a sickening light-headed sensation.

'The termination caused Marina considerable distress,' Bastien delivered in a grim undertone. 'She made her choice, but I don't doubt that the decision cost her. That's the main reason why I didn't persist in arguing my case with Leo. Marina doesn't deserve to have that distressing experience raked up again. So she lied and played victim to look more sympathetic in

Leo's eyes? OK…that was wrong. But *Leo* is the one who chose to believe her story and disbelieve mine.'

Belated guilt pierced Lilah and she felt more nauseated than ever. On one score Bastien was correct. She had not thought through the implications of what she was throwing at Marina. But she was not a naturally unkind or unfeeling person. She knew she should never have referred to so private a matter. She had been cruel, and the shame of that reality engulfed Lilah like a suffocating blanket.

She blundered upright, desperate simply to escape Bastien's censorious gaze and lick her wounds and her squashed ego in private.

She swayed as the room telescoped around her in the most disturbing way. Her head was swimming and her skin was clammy and cold. Not a sound escaped Lilah's lips as blackness folded in behind her eyelids and she flopped down on the rug in a faint.

For a split second Bastien stared at Delilah, who had dropped in a heap on the rug, and then he plunged forward to crouch and gather her up, his brain obscured by the most peculiar fog of something that felt like panic but which he refused to acknowledge as panic. He wasn't the panicking type—never had been, never would be.

He dug out his phone to ring his brother's home and ask for Grace. Leo, mercifully, asked no questions, but Grace more than made up for that omission.

Grace told him quietly and succinctly what to do and Bastien followed her instructions, furious that he had once disdained to take a first aid course, assuming he would never feel the need for such training.

By the time he'd come off the phone and was carrying Delilah down to the main bedroom she was showing signs of recovery. Her lashes fluttered, her head moved, and a faint hint of colour began to lift the drawn pallor of her complexion.

Only then did Bastien dare to breathe again. He smoothed a shaking hand over Delilah's brow to brush back her tumbled dark hair. He had never felt so scared in his life. That knowledge shook him up even more. He had shouted at her, condemned her. And why had he done that?

Maybe I was trying to do something for you, Delilah had said, and the sheer shock value of those words was still reverberating inside Bastien. When had anyone *ever* tried to do anything to improve his life? When had anyone *ever* tried to protect him from the consequences of his own behaviour?

Delilah had been trying to *protect* him.

He swallowed hard. He didn't need anyone's protection. Nobody had protected him as a child or as an adolescent—neither his mother nor his father—and Bastien had learned never to look to other people for support. But Delilah had blundered headfirst into a difficult and delicate situation in a clumsy and futile attempt to straighten out his non-relationship with his only sibling.

Admittedly he had noticed how his wife had pokered up by his side when she'd seenhow the Zikos family treated him. Delilah, he registered in a daze, *cared* about him—in spite of the methods he had used to ensnare her, in spite of all the mistakes he had made.

He snatched in a ragged breath and studied her in wondering appreciation.

'My goodness—what happened?' Lilah mumbled, blue eyes opening to fix on Bastien's lean darkly handsome face. 'Did I faint? I've never done that in my life! I'm *so* sorry.'

'You were upset—and when did you last eat?' Bastien pressed, pushing her back against the pillows when she tried to get up. 'Lie there for a while. Are you feeling sick?'

Lilah grimaced. 'Only a little… It's fading.'

'I'm really sorry I shouted at you,' Bastien said abruptly, a lean brown hand closing over hers, and he was astonished at how easily the apology emerged.

'You weren't shouting.'

'I'm not in a good mood. I was stressed about Anatole and feeling guilty about him,' Bastien admitted, disconcerting her with that confidence. 'I love my father, but I've never been able to respect him, and… and that makes me feel like a lousy son.'

Lilah squeezed his fingers uncertainly. 'No, I think it means you're adult enough to appreciate that he's not perfect and love him anyway…which is good.'

'Do you have a comforting answer for *everything* bad that I feel?' Bastien groaned, searching her anxious features with appreciative golden eyes.

'I doubt it, but you were right about Marina. Dragging that up was cruel… I'm afraid I didn't see it from her point of view, only yours, and I also felt jealous of her, which was even less excusable.' Lilah loosed a heavy sigh. 'I'm ashamed of myself for being so insensitive.'

'You were thinking of me and of my relationship with Leo,' Bastien said. 'But why on earth would you feel jealous of Marina? It's nearly ten years since I was with her—when we were both young and foolish.'

Lilah breathed in deep. 'I'm jealous of anyone you've ever been with. There—I've said it. I've got a possessive side I didn't know I had.'

'Like me,' Bastien cut in unexpectedly. 'I am irrationally jealous when it comes to you, and I've never been like that with any other woman. I couldn't even stand seeing you laughing and chattering with Ciro.'

'*Seriously?*' Lilah prompted, wide-eyed at that confession.

'I've been acting like a madman since I got you back into my life. Unfortunately for you I like my life much better with you in it. In fact, simply waking up in the morning to find you beside me makes me happy,' he bit out with bleak reluctance.

'It…it does?' Lilah was hanging on his every word, wondering why he was talking in such a way. 'Are you still going to be happy if I'm not pregnant?'

'*Diavelos*…what difference should *that* make?' Bastien was bemused. 'If it's not meant to be it's not meant to be and we'll handle it…that is if you want to stay with me…'

Lilah lifted up off the pillows and wrapped both arms round his neck, burying her face against his shoulder, drinking in the familiar scent of his skin in a storm of relief that felt both emotional and physical.

'Of *course* I want to stay with you.'

'There's no "of course" about it,' Bastien countered wryly as he unhooked her arms and gently settled her back against the pillows. 'I railroaded you into my bed and then into marriage, employing every piece of blackmail I had to put pressure on you.'

Lilah treated him to a troubled appraisal. 'I know…
I know you're extremely imperfect and that you've
done dreadful things. I know you manipulated me.
But… I still love you. I shouldn't, but I can't help
loving you…'

Bastien's throat thickened as if he had been slugged
in the vocal cords. 'I don't deserve your love.'

'No, you don't.' Lilah was quick to agree with him.
'But it seems I love you anyway.'

'Which is fortunate, because I'm not going to turn
perfect any time soon, and it's probably best that you
see all the flaws upfront—so that you know what
you're getting in me,' Bastien told her uncomfortably.

Both of his hands closed slowly round hers to hold
them in a grip of steel.

'But I love you too—so much more than I ever
thought I could love anyone. In short, I'm absolutely
crazy about you…so crazy I thought it was *normal* to
waste two years plotting and planning to acquire your
father's business and gain enough power over you to
acquire you as well.'

Lilah blinked rapidly. '*Crazy* about me?'

Bastien lifted one hand to his mouth and kissed
it almost awkwardly. 'Can't-live-without-you crazy,'
he extended in a driven undertone. 'It doesn't matter
if you're pregnant or not pregnant, or even if you can
never get pregnant. I just want and *need* you in my
life to make it feel worthwhile.'

'Even though I go interfering in things that are
none of my business?' she whispered, scarcely able
to believe what she was hearing, while her heart was
taking off inside her like a rocket ship.

'That was just you, taking a typical caring approach to sorting my life out,' Bastien informed her forgivingly. 'You know, in my whole life nobody has ever stood up to defend me or try to protect me until you spoke up today. And when I thought about that… *that* was the crucial moment when I finally realised how much I love you and why.'

Lilah was gobsmacked. 'It *was*?' she whispered.

'I've probably been in love with you since you called me a man whore and slammed that door in my face two years ago…' Bastien groaned. 'I've certainly been pretty much obsessed with *you* ever since then.'

'Obsessed while sleeping with other women?' Lilah derided gently.

'And I couldn't settle for five minutes with *any* of them. Don't blame me for that when you weren't willing to take a chance on me back then.'

Moisture stung the backs of her eyes and she blinked rapidly. 'I wasn't brave enough to dream that something more lasting might come from what seemed to be a very shallow sexual interest.'

'Ouch…' Bastien groaned again, looking pained. 'The minute I had you in my life everything changed, *hara mou*. You make me feel things. And when you're not around… I feel dead, as if I have nothing to look forward to or work for.'

A tear trickled down Lilah's cheek. 'Oh, Bastien…' she mumbled in a wobbly voice. 'You're making me cry. I love you so much, but I'm terrified you'll wake up some day and feel trapped.'

'Every woman who came before you made me feel trapped or bored. You do neither.'

His dark golden eyes burnished with warmth and appreciation, Bastien leant down and claimed a kiss—

a slow, deep kiss that said everything he couldn't find the words to say. She was the woman he hadn't even known he was looking for, waiting for. Her image had been locked in his head for two long years, ensuring that no other woman could please or hold him.

The kiss wakened Lilah's body, sending little tingles into her tender breasts and down into her pelvis. The sound of a doorbell could not have been less welcome to either of them.

Bastien lifted his head. 'I'd better see who that is… Don't get up.'

Lilah slid her legs off the mattress as soon as he had left the room and sped back to the main reception room to reclaim her bag. On her return she passed through the hall, and realised that their visitor was Leo.

When Bastien frowned at her, for being out of bed without permission, Lilah smiled valiantly at both men and muttered, 'I'm going back to lie down, Bastien.'

In fact, she took her bag straight into the en-suite bathroom and removed the pregnancy test she had purchased some days earlier. She had to know one way or the other, she reflected ruefully. Had she not been so fearful that their relationship would be damaged by a negative result she believed she would have done the test sooner. But Bastien's assurances had removed that worry. Furthermore, that fainting fit had roused Lilah's suspicions, because she had never fainted before.

The couple of minutes she had to wait for the result of the test seemed to last an unnaturally long time. When she finally straightened from her seat on the side of the bath she froze, because she saw the result straight away. It had an electrifying effect on her and she wrenched open the bathroom door to yell.

'Bastien? *Bastien?* We're *pregnant*!' she gasped from the bedroom doorway, reddening in dismay when she registered Leo's presence, because she had totally forgotten that Bastien was not alone.

Leo was startled enough by her announcement to break into a grin. He gave Bastien a very masculine punch on the arm and wrenched open the front door for himself, departing at speed to leave them alone.

'Pregnant?' Bastien queried with a frown of uncertainty. 'But I thought you were convinced that you weren't.'

'The symptoms were misleading,' Lilah told him primly. 'Well? You're not saying anything… What do you think? How do you feel?'

'I think I'm in shock. I'm a husband, and now I'm going to be a father, and…' Bastien's beautifully shaped mouth slanted into a wide, brilliant smile as he moved towards her. 'I couldn't be happier.'

Lilah padded towards him. 'Even though it's not what you originally signed up for?'

'I signed you up in an open-ended contract…or didn't you notice that? I *never* promised to let you go, and believe me, I won't now,' Bastien warned her. 'You're my wife, and you're going to have my baby, and I'll never let either of you go.'

'We won't want to be without you,' Lilah swore, rising on tiptoe to close her arms round him. 'I love you so much, Bastien.'

Bastien stared down at her with wondering pleasure. 'I know—and I don't know why.'

'Because you're very loveable,' she pointed out.

Bastien was still bewildered, but he decided that it would be insane to question a miracle. He had done everything wrong and she had forgiven him. She cared about him—*really* cared. When had anyone ever truly cared about him?

His eyes suspiciously bright, Bastien lifted his wife with reverent hands and laid her back down very gently on the bed. 'You need to rest,' he said with conviction.

'No, I need *you*,' Lilah countered, her hand snatching at his to keep him close.

Bastien hung back a step. 'If I join you on that bed, I'll—'

His wife grinned at him, her heart racing, body thrumming. 'Do you think I don't know that? I'm throwing down a red carpet and a welcome mat.'

'In that case...' A wolfish smile tilted his beautiful mouth and he shed his jacket with fluid grace, all power and satisfaction. 'Your wish is my command.'

'Since when?' Lilah quipped, unimpressed by that unlikely claim.

'Since you told me that you love me.'

'I do...' Lilah sighed, breathing in the scent of him like an addict.

Bastien smoothed her hair back from her cheekbone, his burnished dark golden eyes brilliant. 'I really do love you, Delilah...'

Lilah put her sultry mouth to his and slow-burning heat rose inside her, as potent as the happiness she was barely able to contain. Her future was filled with Bastien and the promise of a family, and she was overjoyed by the knowledge.

EPILOGUE

Three years later

LILAH SMOOTHED DOWN her print sundress and studied the sapphire and diamond eternity ring Bastien had given her to celebrate their son's birth. Nikos was a lively toddler, with a shock of black hair and his mother's bright blue eyes. He was also a wonderfully affectionate child, and revelled in the attention he received from his father, who was determined to give his son a secure and loving childhood.

So much had changed during the past three years. Their home base was a London town house, but whenever they needed some downtime from their busy lives they flew out to the chateau in Provence.

The big house was the perfect base for family get-togethers, and Lilah's father, stepmother and siblings were regular visitors. Robert Moore was still running Moore Components, which had gone from strength to strength, expanding to facilitate the number of orders it was receiving.

Within weeks of Anatole's heart attack Bastien and Lilah had celebrated a second wedding in Provence—

a church ceremony, attended by all their family, and followed by a lively party at the chateau.

For a while afterwards Lilah had worked with Bastien as one of his PAs, and that had enabled the couple to spend more time together—particularly when he was travelling a lot. Since their son's birth, however, Bastien had consolidated the various elements of his business empire to enable him to travel less and spend more time with his family.

Grace and Leo had also become steady visitors. It had taken a long time, but Leo and Bastien had finally bonded as the brothers they were. Marina had told Leo the truth about the termination, and Leo had come to see Bastien to mend fences the same day on which Lilah had discovered she was pregnant.

Prompted by Grace and Lilah, who got on like a house on fire, the two families had enjoyed several vacations together, both on Leo's yacht and at the chateau.

Following his heart attack Anatole had lost a good deal of weight, in order to improve his health. He adored his grandchildren, and was a regular visitor to both London and Provence, but his wife, Cleta, almost never accompanied him on those visits. The pleasure Anatole received from seeing his sons finally treat each other like brothers had touched Lilah's heart.

'Sorry I'm late…' Bastien groaned from the doorway, already in the act of peeling off his shirt to head for the shower. 'Nikos and Skippy caught me on the way in and I've been playing ball. Leo has taken my place, even though Rosie has told us that kicking balls is "a stupid boy thing".'

Lilah laughed, because Grace's daughter was extremely clever for her age and often amused the adults with the things she came out with.

She crossed the room to help Bastien unbutton his shirt. 'Happy birthday,' she told him softly. 'Fancy some company in the shower?'

'Is that my birthday present?' Bastien asked hopefully.

Lilah stripped off her dress where she stood, reaching round to unhook her bra. 'No, it's just a surprise. You've been away for three days and I missed you.'

'Missed you too,' Bastien groaned, dropping his shirt to reach for her warm slender body. 'You'll get your hair wet.'

'I'll put it up…'

Lilah moaned under the urgent onslaught of his passionate kiss, sensible matters like her appearance dwindling in importance when it came to reconnecting with Bastien.

'I told Leo we'd be a while,' Bastien confessed.

'Fancied your chances, did you?'

'Always, *hara mou*,' Bastien husked, fighting free of his clothes without once letting go of his wife.

And the passion that never failed to enthral them when they had been apart reigned supreme until they lay in the lazy aftermath, wrapped in each other's arms and catching up on stray bits of news while simply revelling in being together again.

'I love you,' Lilah sighed.

'I love you more,' Bastien murmured, ever competitive.

* * * * *

#3373 SEDUCING HIS ENEMY'S DAUGHTER
by Annie West

Donato Salazar's plan to jilt his enemy's daughter is the ultimate revenge and beautiful Ella Sanderson is certainly sweet enough! But as their fake wedding day approaches, one question weighs heavily on Donato's mind: to love, honor...and betray?

#3374 HIDDEN IN THE SHEIKH'S HAREM
by Michelle Conder

When Prince Zachim Darkhan escapes capture he takes the daughter of his nemesis with him. But while Farah Hajjar is hidden in his harem the line between hatred and desire soon blurs, leading Zachim past the point of no return.

#3375 THE RETURN OF ANTONIDES
by Anne McAllister

Widow Holly Halloran's fresh start is only a plane ride away, until Lukas Antonides—the man she wishes she could forget—strides arrogantly back into her life. As tension mounts between them, so too does that bubbling attraction of old...

#3376 RESISTING THE SICILIAN PLAYBOY
by Amanda Cinelli

Leo Valente is as notorious as the tabloids say he is. But feisty wedding planner Dara Devlin isn't deterred. She needs his family castle for her top client, so she boldly accepts Leo's outrageous challenge to be his fake girlfriend!

REQUEST YOUR
FREE BOOKS!

HARLEQUIN

Presents

2 FREE NOVELS PLUS
2 FREE GIFTS!

PASSION GUARANTEED SEDUCTION

YES! Please send me 2 FREE Harlequin Presents® novels and my 2 FREE gifts (gifts are worth about $10). After receiving them, if I don't wish to receive any more books, I can return the shipping statement marked "cancel." If I don't cancel, I will receive 6 brand-new novels every month and be billed just $4.30 per book in the U.S. or $5.24 per book in Canada. That's a saving of at least 13% off the cover price! It's quite a bargain! Shipping and handling is just 50¢ per book in the U.S. and 75¢ per book in Canada.* I understand that accepting the 2 free books and gifts places me under no obligation to buy anything. I can always return a shipment and cancel at any time. Even if I never buy another book, the two free books and gifts are mine to keep forever.

106/306 HDN GHRP

Name _____ (PLEASE PRINT)

Address _____ Apt. #

City _____ State/Prov. _____ Zip/Postal Code

Signature (if under 18, a parent or guardian must sign)

Mail to the **Reader Service:**
IN U.S.A.: P.O. Box 1867, Buffalo, NY 14240-1867
IN CANADA: P.O. Box 609, Fort Erie, Ontario L2A 5X3

**Are you a current subscriber to Harlequin Presents® books
and want to receive the larger-print edition?
Call 1-800-873-8635 or visit www.ReaderService.com.**

* Terms and prices subject to change without notice. Prices do not include applicable taxes. Sales tax applicable in N.Y. Canadian residents will be charged applicable taxes. Offer not valid in Quebec. This offer is limited to one order per household. Not valid for current subscribers to Harlequin Presents books. All orders subject to credit approval. Credit or debit balances in a customer's account(s) may be offset by any other outstanding balance owed by or to the customer. Please allow 4 to 6 weeks for delivery. Offer available while quantities last.

Your Privacy—The Reader Service is committed to protecting your privacy. Our Privacy Policy is available online at www.ReaderService.com or upon request from the Reader Service.

We make a portion of our mailing list available to reputable third parties that offer products we believe may interest you. If you prefer that we not exchange your name with third parties, or if you wish to clarify or modify your communication preferences, please visit us at www.ReaderService.com/consumerschoice or write to us at Reader Service Preference Service, P.O. Box 9062, Buffalo, NY 14240-9062. Include your complete name and address.

"Are you asking me to pose as your date?"

"What other reason would we have for being in Palermo together? I think it's the most believable scenario, don't you?"

Maybe it was tiredness after the past twenty-four hours catching up with her, but Dara felt a wave of hysterical laughter threatening to bubble up to the surface. The thought that anyone would believe a man like Leo Valente was dating a plain Irish nobody like her was absolutely ludicrous.

He continued, oblivious to her stunned reaction. "You would leave the business talk to me. All I'd need is for you to act as a buffer of sorts—play on your history with his family. Someone with a personal connection to smooth the way."

"A buffer? That sounds so flattering…" she muttered.

"You would get all the benefits of being my companion, being a guest at an exclusive event. It would be enjoyable, I believe."

"Umberto Lucchesi is a powerful man. He must have good reason not to trust you," she mused. "I'm not quite sure I can risk my reputation."

"I'm a powerful man, Dara. You climbed up a building to get a meeting with me. I'm offering you an opportunity to get exactly what you want. It's up to you if you take it or not."

The limo came to a stop. Dara looked out at the hotel's dull gray exterior, trying desperately to get a handle on the situation. He was essentially offering her the *castello* on a silver platter. All she had to do was play a part until he got his meeting and she would be done.

"What happens if you're wrong? If having a buffer makes no difference?"

"Let me worry about that. My offer is simple. Come with me to Palermo and I will sign your event contract for the castle."

She thought about the risk of trusting him. He hadn't given her any reason to trust him so far. But what other possible reason could he have for asking her to go with him?

A man like him could have any woman he wanted, so it wasn't simply attraction—she was sure of that.

He obviously wanted in on the Lucchesi deal very badly if it had prompted him to consider her event. His reaction earlier had been a complete contrast, his refusal so clear. It was a risk to lie to a man like Umberto Lucchesi, but on the scale of things it was more of a white lie. And the alternative meant losing the contract. Losing everything she had worked for.

"If I go with you—" she said it quickly, before she could change her mind "—I want a contract for the *castello* up front."

Leo felt triumph course through him as he felt Dara's shift toward accepting his offer. He'd seen the uncertainty on her face, knew the difficult position he was placing her in.

"You don't trust me, Dara?"

"Not even a little bit."

Don't miss
RESISTING THE SICILIAN PLAYBOY
by Amanda Cinelli,
available October 2015 wherever
Harlequin Presents® books and ebooks are sold.

www.Harlequin.com